G000065413

ENTER THE DARKNESS

"*Enter The Darkness* takes a compelling cast and weaves a web of horrifying folklore around them. It drip-feeds revelations skillfully, dotted with impactful set-pieces. But the real art of this book is in the darkness itself. A foreboding, atmospheric setting which pervades every page."
—Kev Harrison, author of *Below* and *The Balance*

"Fact feeds fiction in this chilling blend of myth and history. Sarah Budd takes you by the hand and leads you into the deepest caves to meet tormented souls in this disturbing tale of ancestral horrors. A fun, spooky, YA-style read for those who aren't afraid of the dark."
—Stephanie Ellis, author of *Paused* and *Reborn*

"A dollop of folk horror, a dash of Druid sacrifice, a sprinkle of pagan ritual, all served up in one of my favourite settings—an ancient system of caves beneath the streets of London. If that doesn't tempt you, what will? Well, how about this...an ancient goddess with the desire to feed on human flesh and her 'servant' who reminded me of the Wicked Queen from Grimm's Snow White."
—Catherine McCarthy, author of Immortelle

"What I really like about Sarah Budd's Enter the Darkness is the claustrophobic oblivion the diverse cast of characters are thrown into. It mixes an authentic, historial setting underneath London with a horrifying piece of folklore that grabs you the second you step into the caverns. Definitely not suitable for those who can't handle being consumed by the darkness."
—Villimey Mist, author of the Nocturnal series

ENTER THE DARKNESS

by Sarah Budd

Edited by Carrie Allison-Rolling, Villimey Mist, and Stephanie Ellis

Proofread and formatted by Stephanie Ellis

Cover illustration by Elizabeth Leggett

First Edition: November 7, 2022

ISBN (paperback): 978-1-957537-10-8
ISBN (ebook): 978-1-957537-11-5
Library of Congress Control Number: 2022948126

BRIGIDS GATE PRESS
Bucyrus, Kansas
www.brigidsgatepress.com

Printed in the United States of America

Content warnings are provided at the end of the book

To Colin, Leon, and Mathilda, for being my light in the darkness

CHAPTER ONE

Date: Spring Solstice, 1,000 BC

Just before sunrise, the boy was brought down into the cave.

Feeling small comforted him. He would never see his mother again though she had put up a worthy fight. He held a clump of her hair in his fist from when she collapsed, finally releasing her grip on him. He would have endured worse than she had to be reunited in her arms, breathing deep her familiar scent of sweet honey and sunshine.

Instead, spiraling smoke of incense crept in through the gaps of the wicker cage holding him. A black mist prevented him from seeing his fate. Fear rendered him senseless, took his screams into the dark and kept his useless limbs trembling. His eyes burned, weeping tears that stained his cheeks black.

Chanting reverberated out of the shadows that surrounded his little body. Forgotten words teasing out the darkness, commanding it to their will. The shadowy figures all around him were hidden in their long-hooded robes. Their summoning teasing out their Queen from the darkness. He hoped it would be over soon.

But the tales have warned him, it's only the beginning.

They say he'll be ground down to black drifting dust. He'll spend eternity billowing along lonely tunnels with the other tortured screaming souls of her underground kingdom.

The wicker cage holding him was dropped to the ground. They helped him across the cold stone floor to the smooth white altar waiting for him. Torches lit his final path, flames flickered in unison to their chant.

It's exactly as the tales told. Bad things await those who break the rules. The Spring Solstice is a dangerous time of year. Darkness loses its fight against the Sun's power, but it always takes one last bite before retreating. Once someone has been picked out by the Druids, they are never seen again. He didn't believe them until his friend, Fiona, was taken. It's been months since he'd seen her.

The altar before him as white as bones licked clean, as smooth as marble. Down in the belly of the cave it is the coldest object his skin has known. Above him sharp jagged flint jutted from the low ceiling. He caught the faint tang of old blood in his mouth. Darkness smothers him.

What comes out of his mouth is barely a whisper, *"No, please."* But the shadowy figures carrying him are strong and unwavering. His skin scraping as he's dragged across the floor. His arms are tied to either side. They stripped him of all he was, leaving him as naked as the day he was born. He couldn't even hide his shame.

The chanting continued. The walls shook with their sound of summoning an ancient one from their lair. The torches couldn't hold back the encroaching darkness any longer. It had grown in strength around them.

All he could see was the darkness, sentient and teeming; so thick he heard its dark undertow rushing around him, prickling his skin. He tasted shadows on his tongue, entering and expanding within his chest as he took his last breaths. In quick flashes of light, faces appeared to him hovering in close proximity, trying to warn him of impending danger. Faces of people he had once known from the village. Those who had disappeared without a trace.

If the elders were feeling kind, they would have slit his throat and let him bleed his way to death. Instead, they made small incisions in the pale undersides of his legs and arms. The darkness fed, his blood drained into tiny channels carved in the altar, collecting drip by heavy drip into a silver goblet that chimed with each drop.

The chanting stopped with a sudden hush. Darkness rushed in to fill every space. The cup was filled, overflowing with his blood.

The robed figures clothed in darkness, bowed down low as they made way in the clandestine underground church. A girl in a long white dress approached the altar.

"Fiona?" he croaked. The boy recognized her even with the surrounding darkness. She still lived, she radiated. It was her potion that saved him from the pestilence. She would help him.

"This is a great honor." Fiona picked up the goblet, taking a little taste herself. The blood staining her lips and teeth. His hope faded when she smiled down on him.

Footsteps came behind her.

A woman emerged from the gloom of the long dark tunnel. A little thing enshrined with legend. When there was light to armor mortal skin, the gathered remain safe.

Her tales only speak of what she comes for. He saw her briefly lit up in the flicker of flames held by one of the shivering attendees. No one had ever told him how beautiful she was to behold. Not in a human way, her eyes blacker than a blind fish living in the deeps. Her skin pale holding moon glow luminescence. So slender she could float away. Was she made of ether and star dust? Her long white hair finer than spider silk, lips of dark wild cherries. He wanted to worship at her feet, she was no ordinary woman. Most women gave life to the world, but this one took it all away.

It is only Fiona who dared approach the deity bringing her the goblet of his blood. The White Lady drank, tasting the boy's warm blood congealing in silver.

Her appetite woken, she threw away the goblet and wiped her mouth with the back of her hand. Her eyes glittered with obsidian.

She only saw the boy tethered to her altar. His bones rattling in heavy chains.

"Leave us," her voice unyielding as stone. The gathered flee, leaving behind a stain of fear swiftly eaten by the encroaching forces belonging to the darkness.

Now it took hold. If only he could have fled with them. She came with a silent rush of cold air as she clambered up onto the altar, joining him. In the pause, he felt her looking upon his body, still hoping for mercy.

"Please, Your Highness, let me live and I'll serve you until my last breath."

He heard her laughing softly as she sat astride him stroking his cheek with sharp jagged nails.

What was she thinking as she looked down upon him? He couldn't see her face, only felt the cold chains keeping him.

There was no time to scream. His eyes opened wide; his breath forced out when her hand came crashing through his ribcage. His limbs fell into seizure, pulling his chains tight. His skin tore with blinding pain but soon he felt nothing. He felt like he was floating away, drifting helplessly into the darkness. Her cold fingers wrapped around his frantic rabbit heart. In one swift pull she ripped it out, warm goo splattering her cheeks. He remained conscious just long enough to hear her first bite into it. He gladly welcomed death.

The White Lady took her fill, feasting on every bite of him, even licking clean the boy's bones; they belonged to her now.

Satisfied and full, she staggered in her blood-stained dress to the wall of carved faces mourning their mortal remains. Admiring her collection, she sang softly as she scratched the boy's sweet face into the soft chalk.

And what a sweet face he had.

People can't always unleash their final scream before they fall into the ever-consuming darkness that cuts into life. The chance is never given to them. The darkness comes too fast, too greedy.

But in her dark underground palace, he could scream forever.

Chapter Two

Garth

Present Day: 20th March, 8 a.m.

Garth shifted in bed trying in vain to recapture sleep until he realized what day it was. *This is it*, he told himself. There was no going back.

Today was Wednesday, 20th March. It was happening. He wished it could be a different day. The day after. When all would be calm.

He'd wanted this for years. He had finally achieved his mission of having a job to be proud of, but he wished he could go back in time. He wasn't ready. But if not now, when? He let out a long sigh and gazed upwards at the ceiling. He was never ready.

This day was going to be even worse than that time he asked Melissa out to the cinema in Year Ten. Beautiful Melissa with her long brown hair and black coffee eyes. A moment of madness in which he thought he'd stood a chance with her because she had been kind and smiled at him after Dean had shoved him up against the lockers before French and spat in his face. Awful and humiliating.

Melissa had only taken pity on him, and Dean had seen it all … Garth shook his head, he needed to rid himself of painful memories to get through today. Now, more than ever, he was determined to leave his past well behind because today, it was his future that scared him the most.

Soon he wouldn't be a young person grappling with the world's harsh economic climate and spiraling house prices. Unless he fought back, he would be nothing more than a written off man-baby still living at home with Mum who cooked all his meals and bought his socks and underwear.

So far, he had nothing to show for his time here on Earth.

By this age, his parents had already married and bought a house. A distant dwindling dream for him. There had never been a girlfriend or a loyal band of brothers to call upon to break the monotony between work and sleep, but he was very good at *Minecraft*.

Alone, Garth wrapped his arms around himself as he sat on the edge of his disheveled single bed, holding his torso tight as he fought off a fresh wave of fear rippling through him and making his insides gurgle.

"I absolutely must not crap my pants today," he said.

Taking a deep breath and staring hard at his carpet, he told himself it would be alright, once he was through it. He genuinely wanted to believe himself.

It was a new day. Maybe this one could be the start of something new? Maybe this time, for the first time in his miserable life, things would start to work out.

***

At 9:30 a.m., Garth pulled up at the caves. He felt sick to his core. He looked around. His left hand stayed on the gear stick and his right gripped tight the key in the ignition, but eventually he got out. His first little victory of his big day.

He stood by his car, put his car keys in his back pocket and slung his rucksack over his right shoulder. Inside was a packed lunch his mum had made. His favorite cheese and pickle sandwiches, two bags of crisps and a Fruit Corner.

He walked forward. On first appearances, the Chislehurst Caves visitor center appeared nothing more than an uninteresting little building left over from the industrious Victorians. No bigger than a classroom it came with a wooden door that was locked each night with a heavy chain. Crouched under ancient oak trees, it was the gateway to an underground world.

Underneath the land of the living was over twenty miles of sprawling dark tunneled veins running under the streets of London. And like the city above, the caves stretched back for thousands of years. Another tiny slice of London's rich history of ghosts and macabre events. The ancient city of London was home to the dead and endlessly wandering.

There was so much more to London's history than the spectral figures seen at dusk patrolling the walls of the Tower of London. The ancient plague pits buried deep under Aldgate. Voices whispering up and down the Greenwich Foot Tunnel, the haunted underground stations of Covent Garden and Bethnal Green late at night.

Ghosts were everywhere, still screaming in the dark London Dungeons, rising from their graves from all cardinal points: Highgate, Nunhead, Tower Hamlets, West Norwood, Abney Park, Kensal Green, and Brompton. London was so old it would always hold more ghosts than living souls.

This was one of the most haunted spots in London and yet most people had never heard of it. Garth always asked himself why the owner was deliberately keeping it hidden from tourists.

CHAPTER THREE

Garth

Present Day: 20th March, 9:45 a.m.

The caves had claimed a powerful hold on him from the very first time he set foot in the underground chambers beneath his hometown in South London.

Garth was five years old when his mother Sandra took him for the first time. He remembered it so well. Today the memory seemed even clearer. It had been summer, the trees were in full bloom, blackbirds sang up high in the beech boughs. The air heavy and overburdened with the scent of flowers and fresh cut grass.

That day he hadn't wanted to be there at all. He'd rather have stayed at home playing with his Lego. That first time was nerve wracking as he walked over the gravel crunching under his trainers. Beneath him were long dark tunnels spreading outwards underneath his town. He feared the ground suddenly giving way with him falling in, never being able to find his way back up.

"Mummy, why do you like going to the caves so much?" he must have asked her a hundred times. She never answered in her usual sweet voice. Instead, she held his hand even tighter and dragged him towards the cave's open mouth. This place was drawing her in without her realizing.

Garth's mum was into the usual activities: baking, gardening, and knitting him itchy jumpers. Except she loved visiting the haunted caves. Garth always got the sense she was searching for something down in the darkness. So keen to him was the feeling she had lost something, or someone so dear to her that she could never let go of the pain the absence caused.

Because of them living so close the caves, it quickly became their trusted refuge, especially after one of his father's fits of rage. It was the one place Dad wouldn't follow them though Garth often wished he would. He entertained visions of pushing Dad into the unending darkness and have him disappear forever. His guilty pleasure that he never told anyone about.

His mother had wanted Garth to see for himself that he was enough. Bravery, she'd said looking deep into his eyes, was carrying on with things even when you felt scared.

His mother held his hand tight and assured him, "Fear is good. Only stupid people don't get scared."

Only clever people knew danger was never far away.

Perpetually afraid of the dark, Garth hadn't wanted to go down there. He didn't like trying new things but his mother promised that if he could handle the caves with the whispering and the darkness, he could handle anything up above. He trusted her completely. She always knew what was best for him.

"It's all around us," she would say. Never elaborating on what *it* was.

By his mum's standards, Garth was very clever. He was always scared. Always felt the danger coming towards him. Always running from the feeling that something was trying to get him.

Plunged completely into a new world his senses lit up like a lighthouse beaming out along a rocky treacherous shoreline. There had been a sudden drop in temperature, the air tasted damp in his mouth. For the first time in his life, fear had loosened its grip on him. Once he was past the double doors he loved being in the darkness of the caves.

There was magic down there, Garth could feel it. After a few minutes of being submerged in darkness, it was in his veins. He heard strange whispers coming towards him. He knew he was being watched.

Not until he went in those caves had he known a true black, devoid of any light. Darker than outer space, more mysterious than the bottom of the ocean, it really was another world that could be reached simply by going through a set of double doors leading downwards.

Garth loved exploring the narrow pock-marked tunnels opening out to wide chambers filled with shivering black air. Down there it was so dark, he was completely hidden, it set him free.

Museum curators keep their collection out of reach but here, his curious fingers could touch anything. His hands ran over the cold damp walls, the texture surprising to his soft skin. He had expected them to be worn smooth over the millennia.

Instead, his fingers caught millions and millions of little dents on the soft walls of the cave, hacked away from ancient axes that carved the very tunnels he now stood in. Tunnels that were hacked through the very earth with sweat and fear thousands of years ago.

Under the cover of darkness, he stuffed his pockets with flint fragments and chalky debris of the miners' pickaxes. They were the first acquisitions in his treasure collection along with his marbles and pennies. There was a real connection here, between him and this cave. One of the few remaining links to a hidden past, long forgotten and shrouded in mystery. He could feel it. A bygone time of when people led a simple but brutal life, governed not by powerful men and their armed forces but by the seasons of the sun, celestial stars, and the Old Ones.

Raptly he listened to the tour guide as he was led along narrow winding tunnels. Here was where the pre-Christians had conducted their underground rituals of worship. Paying homage to the ancient ones. This was no place for modern day Christianity.

He often wondered where the pagans' lost knowledge about life, death and magic had gone when technology sped up the world. Garth learned they believed in life after death. There was a hidden realm parallel to his that they called the Otherworld. A land lying beyond ancient burial mounds, with portals hidden in rolling green hills or clandestine caves.

It seemed to Garth that the world of modern man had declined in intelligence. The ancient Celts had worshipped nature, had respected their forests and oceans, whilst modern people were knowingly destroying their planet in their pursuit of money. He wondered if the Celts had the knowledge to save the planet? Had their secret ancient way of life completely disappeared or merely retreated from view?

He spent many afternoons in the local library as his mother went grocery shopping. But he never found their secrets. His questions remained burning in his head.

On that first visit to the caves, Garth hung back with his lantern allowing himself to become separated from the tour group. He wanted to explore unhindered by himself. There were so many passages on either side of him he longed to run down.

Out of sight he turned a corner feeling his way. The ground gave way suddenly causing him to fall. He used the walls to haul himself up.

There, he made his first dark discovery: a menagerie of odd and grim faces etched into the rock. He stood back and looked up, shining his lantern towards the ceiling. Hundreds and hundreds, if not thousands, of doomed faces lined the walls stretching out into infinity.

They all stared into him. Their eyes following his eyes. They were simply faces carved into the stone, but they teemed with life.

Each one had its own personality. Some of the faces looked down from the ceiling looking ready to pounce. His eyes moved to the faces on the walls, they felt too close to him, their boring eyes made him slip and stumble on the uneven floor.

The tour guide had made no mention of them. Everyone else had walked past without noticing them. He felt honored, that the faces had chosen to appear to him.

One thing the faces all had in common was that they hated their fate; helplessly preserved for eternity in the rock. Haunting eyes full of suffering imploring those who saw them. Their deep hollowed out mouths all agape in horror they could never speak of.

"Mummy, who are they?"

She'd come back for him. If she hadn't been so out of breath, he was sure she would have shouted at him. But she knew better. Instead, she wrapped her arms around him. If only Dad could have been more like her.

He found one of a scared little boy who wanted to be in his mother's arms. Big round eyes imploring for help. Garth had arrived too late to help him. Nobody could help those trapped souls carved in the walls.

"I don't know, sweetheart," she said with a sad sigh, leading him back towards the rest of the group.

"They're all so frightened," he said to himself. Garth knew how they felt and now he didn't have to suffer alone anymore. What was written on their faces was what his dad made him feel. He was always frightened of what his dad would do next. But these faces, they understood his fears.

His fingers had shuddered each time he touched one. There was a power to them. A dark current ran in the caves. He couldn't stop thinking about them long after he had left. Who had taken the time to lovingly carve them all? There was a magic here, he couldn't explain it, he just knew. It made him feel like it was possible to be happy one day. He could find a way to stop all the bad things and people in the world above. He could protect himself if he found a way to harness the magic of the caves.

This was a very special place.

He was brave here, but his fear always retuned the moment he went back up above ground. Horror was everything the world had to offer. The kids at school saw him as a toy. The teachers didn't care what happened in the playground, the loneliest spot on earth.

They loved taunting him until he reached breaking point. He always made sure to be kind to everyone, he couldn't understand why they picked on him. Every day they came, kicking and beating him to see how much pain he could withstand. He wished their punches and kicks would have made him stronger, but it seemed to have the opposite effect, and so Garth steadily withdrew from the world.

Garth got through it because going to the caves always felt like a homecoming. Somehow, he felt he had been there before. His family had always lived in this area. He was sure one of his great grandparents had been a miner. They could have worked here.

There was something about the caves that felt familiar. Instantly he had forged a connection and would until the day he died.

It was the darkness he felt a kinship with, certain it was the same darkness spreading inside himself when he was alone with his bullies subjecting him to pain. Here the darkness took over him, he welcomed its grasp and embraced the cold feeling in his heart.

Once he had surrendered to it, he felt protected. The caves became his church, a sanctuary for his secret dark thoughts.

He would often find the spot where the faces waited for him. Quickly he learnt how to sneak back into the group unaware he had been missing.

Once he was sure he was alone in the dark with his lantern, he poured out all his bad feelings and left them there to be absorbed by the encroaching hound of darkness trailing at his heels. It meant the world having someone who could understand him and was eager to listen to all his problems and secrets. Even all his dreams for the future. He couldn't burden his mother; she had her own problems to deal with.

The silent faces understood his guilt at not being able to stop his dad. His weakness that stopped him from standing up to others at school. His inability to make anyone but his mum like him.

When he came back up, he returned lighter. The darkness listened to his thoughts and silent prayers. It teased out his own darkness, releasing him until he next went to school or home to his father's wrath.

Garth came whenever his pocket money allowed. He told his mum he had made friends who played football in the park on Saturdays. She was so happy he had people to play with. The truth was he came here, to the caves. The tour guides took him in like a stray cat. They let him in for free. Once he was taken down alone.

He longed for the day when he could wear his own khaki *Chislehurst Caves* jacket. He was safe with them. These men were brimming with confidence. They worked down in the belly of darkness all day, every day. Nothing scared them. Garth had made up his mind. That's what Garth wanted to be. He was tired of constant fear of his dad, anxiety over what his mum went through each day. He wanted to be a tour guide and never let anyone hurt him or his mum again.

His dreams felt achievable when he was allowed to help with a tour. Andy let him wear his jacket. It hung down to his knees. It was his job to make sure everyone had a lantern.

"Boy, there's more secrets in the cave than there are answers," the tour guide would tell him as he led him down.

"Secrets? Like what?"

"Well, for a start, what even is this place?" He threw up his hands. "For years it's kept archeologists and historians locked in heated arguments."

"What do you think?"

"Some experts said this was technically a mine and nothing else. Others argued that it had served as a shelter thousands of years ago, whilst others believed it had been a site of ancient worship."

Truth was, no one knew. Or if they did, they kept quiet. Garth was determined to get closer to the caves and find out.

Chapter Four

Garth

Present Day: March 20th, 9:45 a.m.

It hadn't been easy to remember a 10,000-word document on the history of the caves, but Garth had managed it. He'd read it every night before he went to bed for the last three months. Every word committed deep in his memory until it had become a part of him.

What he liked best were all the haunted spots: the underground lake, the old hospital wing, the tunnels that ate sound. There was still so much to explore. It would take him years. He had an idea that when he had found his answers, he'd write a book.

After learning the history of the caves, Garth had quickly progressed to the next stage of training: learning the route of the caves. There were many paths in the darkness but only one was permitted. It was more than geography. He needed to keep his head as he navigated his way in and more importantly, navigated his way out, whilst leading a group of excited tourists. It was more than just dark down there.

He kept his wits about him. The ghosts didn't scare him. The dead can't hurt you—it was the idea of joining their ranks that gave him the shivers. The thought of losing his way in the endless tunnels and never being found alive or dead, was what made his mouth turn dry and his stomach drop. Navigation training was the most fun he'd ever had. Before he was taught the route he had to promise to never ever stray from the route. Never.

Bill, his instructor made him repeat it ten times.

He could do this. Bill was amazed how quickly Garth navigated with authority.

Garth showed great promise. At this critical stage, most newbies failed. Garth couldn't explain it, he could just feel the way it was laid out. There was a pattern to the tunnels if you considered the Druid's Altar the heart of the cave.

It was understanding the darkness that allowed him to figure it out. Something was there beside him guiding him to where he wanted to go. Garth had succeeded where so many other candidates failed. Bill even made Garth wear a blindfold. It had been a joke, but it didn't hinder Garth. He stuck to the route no problem.

No one else possessed a keen instinct for distinguishing what the tour guides called the safe route, where the tourists were allowed, and those passages that were strictly prohibited. Even to Bill.

In the caves there was once a challenge that had started as a bit of fun, until the darkness took over. Now it was forbidden. Many people jumped at the chance to complete the £5 challenge.

To secure the prize, which had been a substantial sum, participants must spend the night alone by the haunted pool. When the caves had been reopened at the turn of the nineteenth century, bones of a young woman were found there. Her culprit never caught, she took out her fury on all who passed by.

It was the same date very year: Halloween. Where it was said the veil between the worlds of the living and the dead were at their thinnest. For one night, ghosts could cross through and wreak havoc. The challenge was to spend the night in the caves, by the haunted pool, where for centuries, miners had refused to venture. All that was permitted to bring down there was one sleeping bag, one radio, one candle and one box of matches to arm themselves with.

Only one person was able to complete the challenge. A level-headed policeman who was used to the darker side of humanity.

One winner in a tradition lasting over twenty years.

Eventually the challenge had to be called off after a guide was seriously injured from unexplained occurrences. His face and shoulder were badly torn. He was rushed to hospital, eventually making a good recovery but after being discharged, he refused to ever talk about what had happened.

His trainer, Bill, was quick to point out that no one could go wherever they wanted, even when they're a guide. There were areas, even on the safe route, that needed to be approached with caution.

Getting lost could be fatal.

Of course, he had strayed. Every day people fall foul of their curiosity and those dark squeezing untrodden paths soon pulled him away from his trainer. Sometimes he thought he heard his name being whispered. The darkness knew his name and along with that tug of being wanted, he followed.

Bill left him at the Druid's Altar as a final test. It was on him to find his own way out. The tunnel he was looking for wasn't there and he took a wrong turn. He'd been led away from the safe route. The ground was unsteady as he tried to back out of the tunnel closing in around him.

At first, the sense of adventure seduced him. He was a kid again breaking free from his mother and seeing the world through his own eyes. He wasn't scared, he knew he wasn't alone down there.

It took moments for him to become surrounded with ghosts. He could feel them brushing past him laughing and whispering as he stood very still. He felt cold fingers spreading over his body, rifling through his warm puffer jacket.

"Let us come back," they hissed.

They dragged him in every direction, their determination as strong as gale force winds, but he held out. He could tell they meant no harm, they only wanted to show him their world.

"Bring us back," their whispers turned to sibilant hisses laced with malice. They were angry now. Garth felt giddy. Now he was messing with forces he didn't understand. One of them pulled his hair with a sharp tug. He slapped them away and got a shove in return. His hood was half ripped off and then they fled.

A black mist crawled towards him from the opposite direction from where the ghosts fled. They were spooked, which Garth found amusing, until he questioned their behavior. What scared a ghost?

The black mist soon took shape. Garth backed away. Darkness seeped out of the walls consumed into the gathering mist. As it grew it sped up. It filtered down the long corridor leading to the altar like fine ocean spray. Before him it assembled itself into congealing pulsating cloud. It moved towards him as if able to see him. It moved fast despite the lack of breeze.

He ran.

"Bill, I saw something." Garth was still breathless when he finally arrived back in the office covered in dust. "Something came out of the tunnel; it was black and horrible."

Bill sighed, pulled at his grey beard, and sat back in his chair. "You went off the path?"

"I heard something."

"Never leave the path."

"But that thing I saw, the black shape It was trying to get me."

"It's nothing for you to worry about." Bill wouldn't look him in the eye.

"Shouldn't we tell someone?"

Bill turned around, pretended to be busy with paperwork. "Why don't you go and do something useful."

Garth left the office, quietly shutting the door.

When he turned up the next day, Garth knew he had the job.

"Garth? What are you doing here?" Bill grabbed him by the shoulders. He was welling up. "I didn't think you'd come back."

"Why wouldn't I not come back?" He winked. It was his turn to well up when Bill handed him his own khaki *Chislehurst Caves* jacket. It fit perfectly.

Jenny, the manager, had already sent out a new job advert to the local newspapers. Not many returned once they got a sense of what else was down there.

Since then, he'd learnt his lesson. Never stray from the path. Listen to the old boys.

Garth remembered what Bill had said with a little shiver. He had been lucky that time.

"With twenty-two miles of tunnels someone can get lost here for a long time, if not forever. There are so many areas where I haven't been, a lot of secret passages where no one goes, and I've been working here for twenty-five years."

But today, Garth reminded himself, he'd be going it alone. Nerves were threatening to get the better of him. He took a deep breath in. Now he worked here, he was one step closer to finding out more about the cave's secrets.

CHAPTER FIVE

Garth

Present Day: March 20th, 9:55 a.m.

Garth could do nothing else but wait in front of the door leading down to the caves. His first tour was about to begin. Jenny the manager had mercifully started him on a quiet weekday. He stood, both feet shoulder-width apart, guarding the doors that led down to the caves.

His right leg tremored. There was suddenly so much to remember. As he stood there, he couldn't recall one single fact about the caves. What if he forgot the route? Was it too late to run?

People gathered in the waiting area. He thought he'd be let off with just a few guinea pigs for his first tour, but too quickly there were people everywhere, full of laughter and excitement, wanting to venture off the beaten path. He counted fifteen people, until it made him too nervous.

They hosted many school trips but not today. Very excitable small children would have grinded on his nerves as well as having to keep a constant head count.

Today he needed order and calm. He didn't have to be perfect. A few mistakes here and there were to be expected on his first day.

If he got through his first tour and everyone left happy, he'd have made a success of it. Just like learning to drive, he reasoned, it would get easier with each tour. After a month or so he'd be able to do it on autopilot.

There wasn't much that could go wrong. He knew his history; he could answer any question thrown at him. He even had a few jokes ready and waiting to be used.

Fortunately, people never went missing down there, he couldn't have that on his watch. The utter shame of messing up that badly was not something he ever wanted to experience.

It was all on him to keep them safe in the ancient clandestine underground kingdom. He took a moment to look at them dotted about. Some of the visitors were talking over hot mugs of tea and coffee, a few others were walking around reading the information boards.

Was he ready for these people to unknowingly put all their trust in him? It really was a tourist trap behind the door.

Even though the doors leading down remained locked and bolted, he still felt the cold insidiously creeping up under his jeans and hoodie. Even in summer you needed your winter coat. He shook his head. No one was wearing their winter coats.

There was a pause in his panic when he caught sight of a young woman sitting across from him, her eyes far away, lost in thought.

Drawn to her and only her, he couldn't explain the stirrings within. He had more chance of finding Narnia than a girlfriend and so after a while other people held little interest for him. He'd long since given up trying to be accepted.

But in just one glance, she'd brought him back from his own little world.

She was startling to him, her effect immediate. Who was she? Why was she here? Straightaway he wanted to talk to her. She had a Celtic look about her, bright skin, curly corkscrew hair almost floating around her and a slight knowing smile on her lips.

Blessed with good looks but she wouldn't realize until age took it away. Someone needed to tell her. Maybe then she wouldn't hide her face so much. Her spilt hair shadowed her features. He wanted to be the one to tell her, he wanted to make her smile.

With a deep breath, he took her in, wanting to capture her face forever with the resolution of a photo in his mind's eye. There was some elusive quality about her that he wanted to know better. Despite her good looks she was an outsider, like him. There was a darkness surrounding her that no one else could see. He wanted to be near her, to know the secret things about her that no one else knew.

What intrigued him the most were those wild bright eyes shining out. There was a light inside her that would never burn out. Garth imagined sitting around campfires with her drinking mead, living alongside her in an endless summer.

He wanted to see the sunrise with her after a long night of heart spilling and dream whispering. He wanted to put his arm around her waist and keep it there.

If only she would look at him, and really see him, not all his failures, his lack of manliness for failing to stand up for his mum and himself in the playground. He prayed she'd see beyond his terrible dress sense. His mum still bought all his clothes, he was dressed like a forty-year-old man in chinos and shirts. He wished she could see inside him, see what no one else understood.

As he continued to gaze upon her and nothing else, her face tilted, her eyes searching all around the room, taking in the black-and-white mounted photos of elegant rock stars adorned with long hair, fur coats and black suede boots. All the greats from The Rolling Stones to the The Who had played here in the sixties and seventies.

She busied her eyes on all the artefacts on display, the old weapons stored here during the First World War, black-and-white photos of the local community who sought shelter in Britain's darkest hour, the Second World War. Each night they came in their thousands searching for shelter from the German bombers.

Garth could see none of these items really held her attention. She was looking for something else. Having the same far-away look his mother had when she came here. He hoped he could help her, because he had failed his mother.

Eventually she came upon him standing by the gateway to the darkness, her eyes dark against her white freckled skin. He was stuck in her gaze. He couldn't steal his eyes away; she held him in place. Under her command.

Where had she been during his cruel school years? But despite the rush, he couldn't think of one intelligent thing to say to her.

He'd missed his chance; spent too long staring at her. Now he looked creepy. Admitting defeat, he looked away. Cursing himself for being an idiot. His dad's voice came uninvited into his head. Why would she ever look twice at a mongrel like you? You're pathetic. Still as weak as the day you were born.

When he lifted his face once more, she had gone. His eyes darted around searching but he couldn't find any trace of her. Of course, she was too good to be real, she must have been a ghost.

Just his luck.

He stepped away from his spot to see if she had gone into the café or through the doors leading to the toilets. She couldn't have disappeared like that.

Screaming in metal agony beside him, the postcard stand turned. There she was, standing a few yards away. Garth had almost walked into her. He breathed out slowly. Had she seen him looking for her? From underneath her dark velvet eyelashes she kept one eye on him, another on the postcards.

It must be now.

"I love my job." He instantly regretted speaking up. Why did he open with that? Why was his voice so high pitched? *Hello,* would have worked better. *Hello, I'm Garth*, he said in his head.

But it got her attention.

She smiled, raising her eyebrows. "I'm Cassie," her voice loud and unwavering.

Cassie had more balls than him, not the slightest bit afraid and frozen when in the company of the opposite sex.

Already he was out of his depth.

"I'm Garth." He pointed to himself. "Are you alone?" Damn it, he sounded creepy.

"Yes." She turned to her left before quickly looking away at everyone else realizing that yes, she was in fact the only lone visitor here. She then pretended to be really interested in the fridge magnets on offer by the till.

"Me too."

She looked at him with new eyes. He could almost hear her thoughts. *Is he trying to be funny or is he really that dim?*

Garth cleared his throat and came a little nearer, not too close to startle her. If he didn't rescue this situation pronto, she was going to write him off as another creepy guy.

"Sorry, it's my first day doing the tours, I'm feeling a bit nervous."

Her eyes bloomed; she moved her body to face him. "You work here? You have a such an amazing job."

"Thanks. I love it here, been coming ever since I was a child. These caves fascinate me."

"Oh, my gosh! Me too, maybe we were on the same tour when we were kids? Do you live locally? I'm just down the road but I live in Bromley now with my … I live alone now."

"Yeah, I'm a local boy from Chislehurst, I'm Garth by the way," he said again, offering his hand.

She edged closer to take it, trying not to laugh.

He was really messing this up.

"Cassie," she repeated, laughing.

He'd made someone smile and laugh. Maybe today would be a great day for him. With a little bit of courage, he was making everything happen for himself.

CHAPTER SIX

Sienna

Present Day: March 20th, 8:47 a.m.

"Fuck off." Sienna gagged when she woke from the stench. Her eyes watered, her nostrils burned, but more pressing was the realization that she had been unconscious for too long. It had been no ordinary slumber. She hadn't been asleep. This didn't happen with alcohol alone.

Even worse was whilst she was under, something had been done to her body. Each night she was plagued with nightmares of a little girl with long brown hair, but she hadn't seen her last night. Though she had one strange memory of an old woman following her out of the bar and whispering strange words that carried in the air.

Not even her thoughts felt like her own. Had someone whispered malevolence directly into her mind? Underneath her conscious mind was an undercurrent of fear and trepidation. Her limbs weren't happy. Her mouth desert dry, yet she still heaved up hot orange bile that tasted like battery acid.

"Fuckety fuck." At least she still had her wits.

She wasn't lying in her bed. Sienna hadn't made it home, but she hadn't gotten lucky either. Everything felt off. Something was wrong.

At first, she was consumed with the shame she'd spent the night in an alleyway, nestled between the dark glass towers of the city where money was made amidst greasy handshakes and dirty deals, where men either triumphed or broke apart. This was her hunting ground, the scene of all her battles and victories.

What a stupid thing to do, she chided herself, acting as her own mother. *Anything could have happened.* Her drink had been spiked. Had she done it by accident? Or was it someone else? Was her prey beginning to work out what sort of person she truly was? That was the last time she was going to Jasper's. She needed a new venue to work from.

But she wasn't in an alleyway. Moving ignited foul cloying odors of damp and rot. Where was her handbag with all her earnings? Where was her phone? She felt around in the darkness until she came to the realization, she wasn't outside. But it was cold like she was stepping out first thing on a wintry morning heavy with lashings of gritty rain and ice.

Beneath her, the floor was wooden and uncomfortable. The texture very similar her wooden laundry basket. Her jittering hands, quickly awoken by sharp pricking splinters, followed the way of wooden canes, feeling them curve upwards over her head forming a lonely human sized tear drop with her trapped inside.

There was no way out.

This had to be a mistake. She raised her arms to see if she could push her way out, but there was nothing. There must be an explanation for this. Sienna moved her legs, despite their strength, unable to completely unfurl. The dimensions didn't make any sense.

She couldn't kick her way out of captivity. The floor moved with her as she shifted to a more comfortable kneeling position, her elbows jammed against the sides. So, she wasn't entirely on the ground either.

As she swung, Sienna rode out the worst of the nausea that swelled. Being trapped in small spaces reminded her of the life she'd left back home. She'd learned to hate the feeling of suffocation. Attempts to spread out her arms and legs did no good in breaking free.

The structure held firm. She was locked within a cage but that was all she could work out. Her head throbbed like storm surge hammering craggy rocks under bruised clouds.

Silence crept up and in.

Sienna closed her eyes, suddenly she was back at the beach, watching the sirens race towards her …

What was happening to her?

She needed to remember every detail of last night. It was a Tuesday, always a quiet night. She had met Hugo; his wife was away with the kids, and he wanted to have fun with Sienna before wifey returned. Hugo was fun, he drank with the zest of a teenager which made her job all that easier. He wanted adventure and mischief. What he got was Sienna.

There's no way he could have known about her—not this early on. They had no mutual contacts. She had made sure of that before she'd moved in. Jasper's was a new venue for her. She never stuck around in the same watering hole long enough for her face to become a regular feature. She'd always been careful.

But someone, somehow, had caught up with her.

Could it have been Edward, her last mark? He was so bitter when he found out she was just another hustler feeding off his bank balance.

He had gone and fallen in love with her, said he would leave his wife and kids to have her forever. He promised to get her a penthouse overlooking the Thames. She'd want for nothing. He would be her loyal servant providing whatever she wanted. He would do everything within his power to make her happy. She was starting to come round but then he lost his job, he stank of sour whisky and beer, his wallet exhausted, and that was it. No, Edward was too distraught to pull something like this off.

Using the force of her entire body, she managed to rock the cage to and fro until she built up a momentum. It wasn't good for her stomach, but anything was better than waiting for the next stage to happen.

She was alone and needed to get the hell out.

There was no screaming rising panic, Sienna was a woman used to surviving on the edge. Women know it's safer to keep quiet, pretend to be dead if needs be. She wouldn't act until she knew more of her situation.

The cage rocked upwards and downwards until she came crashing down onto a floor, her thighs and hips absorbing the impact as she landed. Pain woke up every part of her, but it was worth it—the cage door swung open. It was a simple latch on the other side. Her lucky day.

"Let's do this." She clambered out on all fours keeping low to the ground. She was alone in a dark room. No sign of her shoes or handbag, but who cared for material trappings when there was a door slightly ajar? She could make it. There was no one in the room with her but she kept as quiet as she could just in case.

The open door led her up a staircase of cold white stone and out into a lush hallway flooded with warmth. Her cheeks flushed from the change of temperature.

The royal blue carpet under her muddy feet was thick enough to curl up and sleep upon. The walls of the high ceiling hallway were adorned with stern portraits of bygone aristocracy in heavy golden frames. The house screamed of old money. Where there was money there was Sienna.

Maybe she was in the right place after all.

Her surroundings offered no clues as to who had taken her, but it must have been someone important. Hunger taking root caused her to forget the opportunities all around. If she didn't eat soon, she'd pass out.

At the end of the hallway was her salvation, her path fed into a grand hall full of light coming in from the high arched windows. It would lead her out into the sunshine.

Her bare feet made no sound as she walked quickly. She knew how to sneak out of homes in the cold light of morning.

But this felt different. It wasn't a game. Even her breathing sounded too loud. Anything could give her away. She didn't want anyone to know she had escaped from the cage. People always underestimated her, such as the people responsible for this. But she still wasn't safe. Not until she'd made it outside.

The hallway opened out to a hall; the flooring of black-and-white terrazzo tiles laid in asymmetric patterns like a giant chess board. In the center was a grand staircase of dark wood curling around until it disappeared.

"Whoa." Sienna stopped to marvel. This was everything she had ever wanted. She fought the temptation to sneak upstairs.

A house of this size must be filled with treasures, hordes of expensive and exquisite jewelry passed down centuries through generations, designer handbags and shoes, small antiques easily swiped. She had the contacts to sell it on for an easy profit without attracting unwanted attention.

"Can I help you dear?"

One of the doors to the side opened.

Out stepped a sweet old lady huddled over with age. Sienna held her breath and backed away. She was only a few feet from the front door. She could almost reach the door handle and step out into the morning.

The old woman's head bobbed up and down as if too heavy for her frail frame. Her long hair curled like the actresses in black-and-white Hollywood movies. A housekeeper perhaps?

Her eyes glittered in the light, there was white goo gathered in the corners of her mouth. This grandma was adorable in her floral dress and white apron. She leaned heavily on a handsome walking stick.

Sienna took a deep breath and sighed. She was safe now. Sienna knew this kind woman would probably stuff a handful of cash into her hand if she played this right.

"Yes." Sienna spotted the old-fashioned telephone to her right. She lifted the receiver to her ear. There was a dial tone. "May I use your phone?" She began to dial.

"Of course, dear."

Sienna turned her back to make her call. Rhys would sort her out with a lift. He'd do anything for her, the stupid sod.

The old lady came closer with her walking stick tapping on the floor, placing a cold hand on Sienna's shoulder. The old lady's mouth tightened into a cruel shape. Her collapsed back arched up, straightening with lithe swan-like grace. Her right arm came up high into the air, still holding her walking stick, she brought it swiftly down into the back of Sienna's head.

Chapter Seven

Cassie

Present Day: March 20th, 9:00 a.m.

On that day, it all fell into silence.

Nine months ago, before entering, Cassie paused on the threshold of their flat. She had no idea her life was about to change.

Keys silent, held tight in her hands. Jagged cold metal cutting into warm soft skin. The pause was her daily ritual, trying to guess the intensity of her sister's dark mood. She gathered her strength. She was the oldest twin, by two minutes. It all rested on her shoulders.

It's not her, it's the illness Cassie reminded herself, preparing herself for the storm on the other side.

She slipped in through the front door of their flat. Cassie loved her sister even with the bitterness that grew around them. Theirs was a feral sisterly love that most couldn't comprehend. Setting her keys down into the bowl she knew something had happened.

Their flat was too quiet.

Cassie had quietly closed the front door, sealing herself in the gloom. She closed her eyes, waiting. No approaching storm of footsteps. Even the tinny sound of the television blaring out from their front room was absent. There was no smell of dinner being cooked or burnt. By now there should have been a commotion of activity. There was nothing. Cassie had never come home to nothing before.

On most days, Hayley would come at her, stomping out of the front room, sometimes still in her pajamas and begin yelling mid-sentence. Always angry. Her anger so hot it didn't need a reason. Hayley hated being made to wait for hours to have the chance to punish her sister for whatever crime she had felt wronged by.

But their flat was still.

Cassie had stepped inside a giant pause. Her home paused like a film set before "Action" had been yelled. Their flat was holding its breath. Hayley never went out this time of day. She hadn't been outside for months. Cassie did everything for them both.

Something had happened. The only way for Cassie to get answers was to go to the end of the hallway and step into the bathroom where lavender-scented steam seeped out from under the door, like dragon's breath.

It hadn't felt real. Not until much later.

In the bath was her sister, her Hayley, her twin, an identical copy of her in every way except for the darkness she had been infected with. Now Hayley lay dead in their bathtub in a pool of red, her arms open to the world which had fed without mercy. A razor blade lay beside her.

If Cassie hadn't popped into the local shop for wine, Hayley would still be alive. She would have easily returned in time. She would have hauled Hayley out, called for ambulance.

Had Hayley been waiting to be saved by Cassie or had she really wanted this? The water was still warm. Candles burned all around her, flames dancing on her mottling skin almost making her look alive, but the image was nothing near to being holy.

**

The bathroom remained a tomb long after her twin was taken. They said it was depression. No one blamed Cassie, the only person left in Hayley's life. They said over and over that there was nothing she could have done to save Hayley. There was no way of knowing that would happen.

But Cassie knew that if only she had made more time for Hayley, things would have been different. They could have laughed together rather than constantly fight and bicker. They could have been each other's everything.

They could have still been together.

She should have sensed the darkness taking Hayley under.

If only.

Cassie had lived in fear her sister's madness would take her too if she spent too much time with Hayley, and because of that she refused to get too close. She had thought it sensible and correct to distance herself, thus spurring Hayley to snap out of the dark spell and become normal again. After all, she was her twin, and Cassie was fine.

Someone had to stay strong and pay the bills.

They had the same face and genes. Their lives should have been as identical as their bodies. Sometimes it's harder to be happy, it takes more courage to say no and change your life when it starts to go awry. Cassie realized in life you got back what you put in. Moaning and misery got you nowhere. But still, how had the darkness gotten her sister?

Life hadn't been the same since her sister left.

Was Hailey finally at peace or was that dark undercurrent still breaking inside of her, wave after wave?

Now it was Cassie who ignored the outside world. The door was shut, the curtains closed. Cassie hid away in their flat. Just like her sister had done.

The darkness had gotten her after all. First Hayley, then her.

Within these four walls, the wallpaper peeled. Damp swelled in the corners; the windows were never opened. Her tears stayed with her. Still, she couldn't leave, couldn't face being outside even though Cassie knew she was being watched within the flat. Now she understood.

Cassie refused to believe Hayley, had gone away. Something of her remained. They would always be sisters and when those strange images came into Cassie's mind of endless dark tunnels, screaming faces carved into soft white rock, the feeling of being hunted forever more, she knew it was Hayley trying to communicate with her.

Every night she woke up, certain she had been screaming. Fear and darkness had taken hold of her too. Now it was her turn. Cassie had become convinced that Hayley was never more than a few feet away.

What was it Hayley wanted? If there was anything she could do to help her sister, Cassie would do it. Some nights her throat grew sore, tears spilled onto her pillow as her legs shook with rage and hurt, but Hayley never answered. She was always being watched but the surrounding perpetual silence made her feel ignored too. Why wouldn't Hayley answer, give her a sign that she was there?

Hayley's continued presence made it seemed like she wanted to talk, she wanted to stay with Cassie, but she couldn't make contact. Her determination to remain had made it feel to Cassie like they had grown closer but there was still a barrier that separated them. Cassie knew the boundary that cut them off from one another was thin, something that could be crossed. She needed to get closer to death to live again.

Cassie wanted so badly to talk with Hayley. She needed to know why. Could she have done more, was there anything that could have been done to stop her sister's obliteration?

In another world, not so far away, Hayley could be sat with Cassie on their sofa watching *Made in Chelsea* and munching down huge bags of cheesy crisps. It was a stupid mindless show, but they loved it. The only thing they had in common.

It was during an empty afternoon when sunny skies became overwhelmed and darkened with sudden rain. Big fat blobs that obscured the view from her window. Cassie remembered their old childhood pact forged under dark clouds on a rainy Saturday afternoon, down in Chislehurst Caves near where they lived.

The very day when Cassie first noticed Hayley's preoccupation with the darkness that had taken her as a bride. Yes, she thought to herself, certain now that was when Hayley changed.

Hayley was rapt when the guide told them of the ghosts that dwelled underground in the many never-ending passages that made Cassie feel sick and dizzy.

Something had been switched on inside her. Hayley talked about those ghosts for weeks to come until their mother told her off and sent her to her room.

Cassie had never liked that sort of thing, but Hayley loved it. That was when Hayley had turned away from the living to be closer to the dead.

Hayley was beside her as they walked past the old Druid Altar. Cassie had shuddered on sight of the white slab of rock. The indents worn into it did match a human laying down, and even though the tour guide joked that it probably wasn't an altar, she knew it was. There was a stain in the atmosphere. She turned to see if Hayley felt the same. But she wasn't there.

Cassie swung the lantern around in the gloom but could not find her. She grew worried. The adults had turned left, their echoes growing distant in the darkness.

"Hayley?" She walked along a very long dark tunnel. "Hayley where are you?"

Cassie had no choice but to walk further into the gloom.

Something was watching her.

The air was especially cold. She stumbled on the uneven stone floor.

As the lamp swung wildly, she saw something. It was Hayley, stood very still, poised like the mannequins in the old underground hospital they had passed earlier.

"Hayley?" Cassie moved the lantern closer. Hayley stared on with dull glassy eyes. She didn't see Cassie standing there, couldn't feel Cassie's breath on her face. It looked as if she were hypnotized. Cassie turned around. There was no one else she could see in the tunnel with them.

"Girls!" Their mother came thundering down the dark tunnel. She skidded to a halt when she found them. "What on earth are you two doing?"

Hayley turned and silently walked out, leaving Cassie to explain. But even when they went back up after the tour, Hayley was different. She didn't run around like she used to do. She became meek and pensive. She turned inwards and shut out Cassie. Until then they had been so close.

It broke Cassie's heart that no one else noticed the change in her sister. Her parents said she was being silly. It was only now that Cassie remembered what Hayley had said to her in the caves.

"Hey Cassie, when we're dead, lets come back and haunt this cave!" She had squeezed Cassie's hand so tight, sending a shiver of mortality running up her spine. She'd been ten years old, too young to realize death would one day come for her. She thought she would be a kid forever.

Now, Cassie needed to know whether ghosts were real. If so, there was a chance she could find Hayley. Maybe she was already here by her side, or had the madness come for her too?

She hoped this cloistered feeling around her was Hayley, not something else. Had Hayley opened a doorway in that bathroom when she left this world? There was no one to talk to who would know about this.

Maybe the best way was to address the source.

She trawled endlessly on the internet reading witness accounts, she went to her local library, surprised at how many books had been written on the subject.

Chislehurst Caves had a long tradition of ghosts. There must be something down there that allowed the dead to remain. She had recently discovered the caves ran under their flat like a vein permeating their town.

Those caves had always been there in their lives. Now it was making its mark. Could Hayley really be down there? Waiting to talk? Could she release Hayley from her suffering?

The only problem was staying there long enough to coax her sister out of the shadows. Hayley had always been stubborn. Cassie knew she would have to stay there overnight, in the darkness, completely alone. There was no other way.

At least she wouldn't be the first person to attempt it. But the stories of those who had tried hadn't inspired her with confidence. They had been brave whereas she was not. The stories of the £5 challenge had terrified Cassie, but she needed to go and find her sister. Hayley needed her help. Cassie was not afraid of the darkness down there, only the emptiness that had swallowed her whole since her sister's passing.

Her research had thrown up an interesting idea which Cassie leapt on. The caves were no ordinary caves. They were more than just narrow twisting tunnels.

There must be a portal down there.

After deciding on what needed to be done, she took the day off work and packed a small rucksack of supplies. She had every intention of leaving once her mission was completed.

It hadn't been planned out in advance. Cassie had woken up one morning. Even after a night of sleep she was tired of living in such close proximity to death. She wanted to be in the real world again, not in this entombed flat.

Bringing a sleeping bag with her would have been too obvious, it would have provoked questions. So, she left it at home and packed a warm hoodie instead. She wouldn't be wasting her underground time with sleeping.

As an afterthought she packed a few chocolate bars into her rucksack and a week-old half-drunk bottle of water from her handbag.

Finally, this felt the right thing to do. She left her flat with a purpose in her walk. She was on a path to something, and anything was good right now, a break from the stalemate.

There was something she needed to confront; she knew the darkness held it in its hands like a poisoned apple, down there, waiting for her.

CHAPTER EIGHT

Garth

Present Day: March 20th, 10:00 a.m.

Cassie stayed close to Garth when he took her and the rest of the group down into the caves. His first tour. He had a good feeling about it.

The double doors, held together with padlock and heavy chain, opened inwards. What greeted them was a dark stare, a watchful gaze sifting through them.

An icy breath filled up the waiting room.

People braced themselves, momentarily held in silent awe as they stepped over the threshold after handing over their pink ticket stubs.

Garth smiled as he beckoned them into the mouth of the cave; it was their time to be nervous. His nerves were melting away. Some looked behind them back to the light as Garth shut the doors sealing them in.

Now there was no going back.

The owner shouldn't let just anyone down here, especially when they didn't know the risks involved, Garth thought to himself, the darkness beneath held many secrets. His co-workers clearly knew more than they were letting on. Garth would never forget their stunned faces when he showed up the next day after seeing some strange things down there. He was yet to understand how the caves were ever opened to the public. But he would keep them safe.

The damp air tasted of chalk and wet cement. They followed Garth in single file, their feet trudging uncertainly through low ceilinged tunnels pockmarked with sharp juts of flint. The cave swallowed them whole, taking them to a different world. Each person felt alone in the darkness surrounding them. Old thoughts coming to the forefront of their minds. The mood turned quiet, everyone looking inward. The land of the living up above becoming a distant memory all apart from his dad.

The darkness held all the memories Garth wished he could forget. Sometimes they were returned. He felt his father was right beside him, whispering into his ear that he was a good for nothing waste of space who'd never amount to anything.

But today, for the first time, he was able to put those thoughts aside. Garth grinned. All because of her. He was the leader of this expedition with a beautiful girl by his side. He could be anyone down here. He was Doctor Who and Cassie his adoring assistant. In her eyes, he was a somebody.

Cassie was helping him more than she would ever know. With her attention locked onto him, Garth blocked out all the others. He focused on her. Everyone else was lost to the darkness. He wanted her to hang off every word he said as if it were gospel. He wished it was just them in the caves. He didn't want this to ever end.

This place made him feel invincible.

Afterwards. When he would lead them back, she'd leave through those doors and walk out into the sunlight. What if he never saw her again?

He couldn't let that happen. He had to do something, anything, he had less than an hour in which to create a lasting impression. A good one. Though he'd never been anything other than a loser, he was going to have to pretend to be normal for an hour. He clenched his fists ready to battle against loneliness.

"I can do this," he whispered to himself.

He watched her comb the damp chalky walls with her fingertips. She didn't know it, but she was smiling. He suspected she might even be the one when her fingers found an old face carved into the smoothness. Its touch forced her hand away. She almost lost her footing as loose scree scrambled under her trainers.

This wasn't part of the tour. Nobody ever took any notice of his companions but she had. They hid in the darkness just meters away from the safe route. Another excuse to stand close to her. He shone his Turbo 500 torch over the face carved into the wall so she could marvel at the hollowed eyes that stretched wide with fear, its mouth frozen mid-wail.

Cassie stopped smiling. One of the faces looked on into the darkness, its grave features eroded by damp. It detested being under the scrutiny of torchlight and Garth imagined he could see the face slowly changing from pained to vengeful the longer he looked at it.

There was something that made him want to run, even venturing off the path, just to be away from the silently screaming face. He backed away fearing he might feel its breath against his skin. The hollowed-out pits for eyes deepened the brow furrowing against the light. Was the mouth stretching wider? He seemed to think so.

"That's so creepy." Cassie stepped back, pushing past him to get away from it. He reached out a hand to steady her. She didn't flinch from his contact.

A first, a great big milestone to not have sent a girl running off into the hills when he came near them. Did that mean she liked him? Enough to hand over her phone number afterwards? Garth smiled, pushing back his shoulders to make himself appear taller and stronger.

Everything was happening at once; the curse on his life had lifted. He'd gotten his dream job; could he find his dream girl too? All these achievements in one glorious day. He grinned. Life could be so easy when it was in a good mood. He wanted to follow her but decided instead to hang back. *Play it cool*, he told himself.

Garth moved his lantern up and down, staring once more at the face to see if it would change again. He dared himself to keep looking. He wondered who the face had belonged to.

He'd kept a careful watch over them since he was a child. Their number still grew. Somebody was still doing it. He was still no closer to knowing who had carved it.

He had never noticed this one before. It was new. There was something familiar about those features. It was as if they had met before. The bone structure was like someone he knew but he couldn't recall who it was. Or maybe it was what the face was doing that unsettled him? Was this the expression people made when they realized they were dying? Their eyes forever open wide. An image came to him of a young woman being forcibly held under water watching their last breaths escape them as bubbles rising to the surface. He felt a pang of sadness.

Cassie hung back from the rest of their group, watching him staring at the gruesome carving in the wall. He felt her stiffen when she realized the true scale, there were thousands of faces, all watching her.

Absently, she grabbed his arm to pull him away from the face. She laughed nervously when she realized what she'd done, relaxing when Garth broke into an easy grin. How could someone like her be falling into his lap like this?

"Let's get you away from here. It's best not to stare at them too long."

"Please."

He moved on leading his group further into the darkness filling every crevice. He was just getting started. This cave was his life's work. There was so much still to be discovered and it gave him thrills.

"Okay everyone, from this point as we start to descend the tunnels will get smaller, so watch your heads."

"Where do these tunnels lead to?" one of the visitors asked.

"Good question. We can't be sure these tunnels even end. No one has been able to determine that. As you get deeper in, I've been told they become more like wormholes. There's less air down there too. We'd need professional exploration teams to find out. But it's never been done."

"Couldn't you do it?"

"I would if they let me." He grinned. "We're turning right at the end of this tunnel."

"Let's hope we're not going down a wormhole," someone whispered.

As he whistled, he planned for a way of sneaking Cassie down here after closing time for a date. She clearly loved the caves as much as he did. He could talk for hours on the subject.

Would a bottle of red wine, a picnic of cheese and pickle sandwiches, salt and vinegar crisps and red rose scented candles be too much? After all these years, he'd survived, and now he had found her.

He no longer felt like the lame Garth up above who stumbled with every little life obstacle. His dad had hated him, he was bullied at school, too poor to go to university. The same Garth who never had a girlfriend because he spent his wild teenage years hiding in his bedroom playing computer games and reading Andrzej Sapkowski.

Things worked differently in these cavesEverything was changing he could feel it, after today he'd be a different man.

CHAPTER NINE

Garth

Present Day: March 20th, 10:15 a.m.

The caves made it easy for people to forget themselves. When the darkness called forth, it took all souls within reach. Wrapping their tendrils tight, its flock was brought into a reality no mortal could ever comprehend, one that made most people afraid. For a few, the opportunity filled them with wonder.

Garth watched his group taking in lungsful of damp and chalk. The first time he did that it left his tongue fizzing with the taste of minerals and old dank air. It didn't make him feel sick, instead it revitalized the old ancient being within.

Darkness pervaded, even with the sparse lamps dug into the soft chalk walls, his group realized how powerful the sun was to banish all this underground. How far mankind had advanced since the discovery of flame and magic. They could appreciate early man's gratitude for their guiding light within the dark of the universe.

After a brief safety talk on how to use the old-fashioned kerosene lanterns, he handed them out.

"Remember guys, only touch the handle, the other parts get very hot." The flames inside danced as he handed them out.

He took them further in. The change in atmosphere so sudden and swift he stopped and waited for them to acclimatize. The sound of silence was shocking. One by one they realized the arcane magic contained here. Garth found it beautiful to watch his group members having a mind-altering experience without the need for psychedelics.

Garth would see them through, after learning this route for months, helping out with important site maintenance, checking the displays, making sure the lights were all working properly after hours. He thinks he knows it well.

He stood by the map painted during the seventies feeling less like Indiana Jones and more a schoolteacher waiting for his group to coagulate around him. He loved watching their faces feeling exactly as he did on his first day here. They knew they had stepped into something special.

They were nervous, vulnerable to the unseen darkness surrounding them. They relied on him. In front of him was a big map of Chislehurst Caves divided roughly into three sections as complicated as a plate of spaghetti.

He took in a big breath. This was it.

"Welcome to Chislehurst Caves." He paused and held up his finger. *Keep it together mate,* he warned himself. His right leg started to twitch again. *You got this.* "Actually, that's a lie. This is believed to be a mine, thousands of years old. If you look at this map you can see that Chislehurst Caves are divided into three main sections, Saxons, Romans and Druids. These caves are said to take up an area of twenty-two miles when it's all lined out, but to be honest no one really knows how far they go due to its age; people have been mining on a big scale here since ancient times. "If you like to gather round …"

He gave more details about the section he liked the best, the Druid section, the oldest and least explored area. In some parts the tunnels were too narrow and low to put in lighting. It was unclear where they led, they kept going further down despite the lack of mineral deposits.

No one went to those parts. They didn't say why. He'd only been told to avoid that area. After seeing that strange black mist near there he knew had stumbled on something he wasn't supposed to have seen. What was it Bill was keeping secret from him? He had to find out.

There are legends that say the Druids at one point lived down here, willingly. Even more, but unsubstantiated rumors, that they performed rites of blood magic and human sacrifice. Nothing had been investigated fully; the owner, an old woman named Fiona, disliked archeologists coming down here.

She didn't want the place disturbed.

"Most people think of the Druids as peace-loving hippies, but in fact, back then they were bloodthirsty and unforgiving whenever a crime was committed. Men, women, and children would be burned to death in a wicker cage for their wrongdoings—no matter what act they committed. Yeah, just like the Wicker Man. No trial of course. It was said they sacrificed humans down here to their gods and on this tour, I'll be taking to you to what was rumored to be their altar."

He noticed that everyone had become quiet, staring at him in wonder, no longer a disappointing young man but the keeper of the underworld.

He chuckled to himself. He was a new man.

"These caves were also used as a music venue attracting the likes of The Who, Hendrix, the Stones, and our very own local legend, David Bowie. It was a lifeline during World War Two for locals seeking shelter from the bombs coming across the Channel. Follow me."

He settled into his performance. People laughed at his jokes and asked him questions which he knew how to answer and impress. He walked ahead pointing out the sleeping accommodation, long bleak tunnels that had been filled with three-storey bunk beds. Nearby was a makeshift hospital run by a doctor and nurse team. It was basic but sufficient when above ground was too dangerous.

"For those too frightened to sleep, there was an underground church which had been consecrated by a local priest. They would take their place under the makeshift white wooden cross penetrating the gloom. Many people must have prayed here during Britain's darkest hour, praying for the safe return of their sons from war, for those who had fallen and for their own lives."

Garth kept a head count whenever they paused at points of interest; the next stop would be the Druid's Altar.

Beside him, Cassie stayed close. She was his good luck talisman. He could feel her smile against his skin. If she liked him before the tour had started, she definitely liked him now. His first day was getting off to a great start. He guessed at what her hair would feel like if he were able to run his fingers through it. Then he stopped, he was getting weird, and this was why he'd never had a girlfriend.

But on the other hand, is it also because he'd never gone for it, to follow his dreams and desires with pluck and courage? He'd always backed away; never thought he was worthy of them.

As they walked, he noticed she was so close to him their hands were almost meeting. Something was happening here.

"This place is amazing. I never knew about the Druids. Did they really know how to use magic?"

"I believe so, though there's little evidence to prove it. I'm certain they were incredibly intelligent in the absence of modern science."

"Imagine knowing what they did …" Her voice began to trail off.

"So, what brings you down here?" he asked, finding anything to preserve their time together.

"Research." She was hesitant to expand any further.

"I could help." He paused. "We could get a drink afterwards. I know everything there is to know about these caves."

He stopped himself. It just slipped out. He shouldn't be asking out women like this on his first day. She might lodge a complaint. He could lose his job before the day was out. Was he being inappropriate?

She looked across but had no time to answer him. The others came up close, asking more questions about the Druids and their sacrificial rituals. She looked away, saying nothing.

That's a no then, he thought, glad that the darkness hid his face.

He was already mourning for the life he would never have with her. What had he done wrong?

CHAPTER TEN

Cassie

Present Day: March 20th, 9:45 a.m.

That Wednesday morning, Cassie arrived at the caves. Her chest began to feel tight. Very little of the visitor center had changed. Walking over to the little hut brought back memories of the dark pact Cassie had foolishly made with her dead sister. Was this why Hayley's ghost refused to leave Cassie's side? A pact is a pact.

They had been happy once. Cassie and Hayley. Identical twins devoted to one another. Hayley used to laugh as easy as water trickling downstream.

Cassie had always thought Hayley would be the successful, happy one, she moved through life like a butterfly until things began to change ...

It all started here, Cassie thought. A strange thought came to her, *it could have so easily been me.* She steadied herself, remembered the plan, why she was here. There was important work to do.

Inside, Cassie entered the café, choosing a juice. She needed sugar today. To her right she stared at the table in the corner. She had sat there sharing cheesy chips with her sister. There had been a fight over the greasiest cheesiest chip. She dabbed at the corner of her eyes with her sleeve and moved away.

Out front, before the double doors leading down, were old dark wooden church pews and the air of excitement. People waiting to descend to an ancient underworld.

She took a seat, away from everyone else, holding her ticket tight in her grasp. Everyone around her seemed so normal, so ignorant of what awaited them all.

It's inescapable, no matter how we choose to live—in the end we all go into the darkness. Every single one of us. Except it had already found Cassie. It was dragging her down. She couldn't fight it forever.

She felt more alone, this was a place for families.

Today it was mostly couples and retired people looking for a few hours of entertainment. This was just a fun day out. Not a place for the bereaved searching for the voices of their dead kin.

There was a young man standing guard by the door, hands clasped in front of him, looking as nervous as she felt. Cassie shook her hair over her face, regretting that she wasn't wearing any make-up. Not that someone like him would notice her. He was tall, blonde, and handsome. What she liked most of all were his big brown eyes devoid of malice. He was one of those elusive nice guys she had been looking for all her life. She was also certain he would have a girlfriend.

When he caught her eye, she held it. Now was not the time, but she was reluctant to look away. Someone other than her dead sister was paying her attention.

For a moment she felt like she ought to, a young single girl ready to meet the world. They shared a strange similarity she could never explain. He was there with her, in the shadows. Dark revelry dancing around them both.

She walked over to the merchandise on sale keeping him in her periphery. He was still watching her, she felt it. She looked up only for him to look away too quickly. Embarrassed he got caught.

She grinned. He grinned back.

"I love my job," was all he could think of. He was weird, but so was she.

"I'm Cassie." She stopped short of looking to her right where her sister always stood in life waiting to be introduced. Hayley would have thought he was hilarious. She'd be nudging Cassie so hard in the ribs right now if she were still alive.

First, he looked behind him, he must have thought she was talking to someone else. Then he became very flustered when he realized she was talking to him.

"I'm Garth. Are you alone?"

Was he looking around for a boyfriend?

"Yes," she said, after consideration. It was too early to bring up her dead twin sister.

"Me too." He wasn't talking about the caves.

The tour began. He unlocked the doors and held them open, like he was doing it only for her. He watched her as she passed by into the tunnel where the darkness was ready to bite. Fear ran through her, but she had never been so sure in her entire life. She felt safer with him by her side.

The darkness was deeper than she remembered. Her skin even underneath her clothes, was porous to its touch. Her arms noted the coldness first, from there it gathered momentum brushing against her legs and creeping underneath her hoodie. It wanted to hold her close, wanted her to let it be absorbed under her skin.

It was alive.

Coming down into the caves put her face to face with the feeling that had been stalking her.

It was real, this cold feeling of dread, had been running underneath her whole life. It had attached via her grief, her dark thoughts and the only way to survive was to get utterly lost in its maze.

Except she didn't feel as alone as she should have done. Garth was her kindred spirit. Trying to fit in to the world when even he knew deep down, he didn't belong. He was more comfortable by himself. She preferred books to people. Maybe they could be completely at ease together?

Cassie wanted to reach out, take his hand in hers, tell him it's okay to be like that. They walked together so closely. She thought maybe he liked her back, but maybe he was just being friendly? It was his job to make sure everyone had a fun time.

Me and you, we're the same.

Would that be crazy talk if she told him that? For the first time in her life, she was losing all her awkwardness to a deep desire to connect to someone. They were becoming different creatures down here, shedding their skins to become who they wanted to be.

Deftly he fell in step beside her, nudging her to get her to look up at him. He grinned to assuage her nerves. How could he have known what she was feeling?

When she was a child, her father would always threaten to send her and Hayley down here when they were naughty. He said many years ago bad people would be left here to get eaten by monsters. Their mother would clip him round the ear for it, but he was adamant it was true.

The chalk walls of the tunnels were soft, like teeth after too much fizzy pop. Unused to the sensation, Cassie ran her hand over them until she touched upon a ripple of shapes causing a stabbing pain in her chest. She stopped to look with her lantern.

No one else noticed the face carved into the wall.

It was lying in wait for her. The face stared back, aware of her attention. She looked closer and took a big breath. The face was actively looking at her. It had recognized Cassie.

When they locked eyes, the face carved into the wall changed, the protruding bottom lip jutting out. Hayley made that exact face when she couldn't get her way.

That was how Hayley always looked to Cassie. In her last years she was always moaning about something or other. It became clear she could only feel joy and fulfillment through her misery and suffering.

It looked too much like Hayley.

"That's so creepy."

Garth was close behind, his breath coming down her collar bone. She pushed past him to get away from Hayley's face carved in the wall. She looked up, why were there so many faces?

Garth led them further in, away from that horrible face. She smiled because she remembered this bit standing by the huge map of the caves, a series of little corridors sprawling outwards like a huge nest.

Garth relayed the history of the caves. What came first, Chislehurst or the caves? She liked watching him storm through the cave excitedly like a little child. He was tall and strong looking but underneath she could tell he was a kind soul; one she would love to wake up next to. She quickly blushed and looked away in case he could read her thoughts.

Afterwards they continued through the caves, she walked beside him again, hoping he hadn't forgotten her already. Everyone loved him and she shocked herself with a pang of jealousy wishing it were just the two of them down there.

"That was amazing. I never knew about the Druids."

"So, what brings you down here?"

"Research." She hesitated to say more. He wouldn't like her so much if he knew the truth.

"Could I help?" He changed track. "We could get a drink afterwards. I know everything there is to know about these caves."

No one had looked at her like he did for an awfully long time. Within his gaze she was cherished. He would go to the ends of darkness for her. No had ever come as close as he had. She rattled between being nervous and calm.

There was something happening here. Cassie was about to say yes until someone else approached to ask Garth a question. She had wanted to stay with him, but she had no choice in the matter.

Now was her chance.

CHAPTER ELEVEN

Garth

Present Day: March 20th, 10:30 a.m.

He led them deeper, to his favorite section within the caves. What people came to see—the Druid's Altar.

After centuries, the sight was still awe inspiring. When visitors came to pay their respects, everyone fell quiet at the sight of the majestic stone altar carved into the rock looming out of the black.

The power of the caves was still felt. When they took their place in front of the altar, they could see all those rumors were true—despite what anyone says. It's encoded in DNA, the secret written history of ancestors.

Everything felt different here, a ghostly residue of the past coated everything. One could almost hear the low thrum of druidic chanting, the raising of their magic, the smell of their incense and the slicing of the dagger across soft quivering skin.

They congregated around him. Garth angled his torch towards the long corridor stretching behind them, pushing back the darkness. Their eyes followed. The procession route was dark as far as the eye could see. Never ending. They had reached the end of the mortal world; beyond, a different sphere existed.

"Imagine the Druid priests slowly walking towards you as you wait to be sacrificed." Even he got chills in his belly when he contemplated what it would be like to venture inside the oldest and least known part of the cave.

"This is the longest tunnel. It was believed to be the route of procession for the Druids who came here to carry out their clandestine worship unhindered. None of us tour guides and staff members can go down there. Not even the seasoned tour guides who've walked these paths for years. It's all too easy to get lost the further in you go. It gets very narrow and tight. Thousands of years ago, people were a lot shorter and smaller." He winked at an overweight tourist and the crowd erupted in titters.

Garth pointed to the altar. "There's no concrete evidence to suggest this was ever used by the Druids but if you look carefully, you can see where the stone has been worn smooth, and here in the middle the depressions do in fact resemble a figure lying down. Imagine how many people must have lain here to create that effect? Here is where their heads could have lain and see this channel carved in by the head? It was claimed to have been where the blood was siphoned off for use in dark magic rituals. You can come up and feel for yourselves. Don't be afraid, I'm not going to sacrifice anyone." He paused and grinned. "Today."

Most laughed at the thought of human sacrifice. A few grew very nervous. Thankfully, it had been left in the past but when they came up to place their hands on the cold stone altar they fell into silence—realizing they were standing in the spot where it had gone on. In a different life it could have been one of them chosen for sacrifice.

"We're going to have a bit of fun!" He clapped his hands making a few members jump. They were too confused to protest as he collected their lanterns. He enjoyed the startled looks on people's faces.

"I'm going to show you what true darkness is. Very few people get to experience this in our modern world. Bear with me as I gather the lanterns which I'll take around the corner. I want you to stay very still and quiet. You're going to get a feel for the true darkness of this place. Now don't worry, I'll come back and save you. If anyone thinks they'll find it too much to handle, you're welcome to follow me."

No one followed.

When he switched off his torch, the last source of light, he heard a collective gasp. All the lights had been extinguished. Garth felt the darkness clamber on his face, so dark it felt heavy, a substance of black fog.

This was his favorite part of the tour. He loved this bit when he was young: the mixture of fear and relief.

When submerged in complete darkness one loses all sight and see strange things materialize. Strange symbols, images of faces or dancing patterns of light that they know can't be there come out. But yet it feels so real. Too quickly people find themselves in a position of being unable to judge what is real and what is imagination, and whether there is a difference between the two. Sometimes they see people from their past, those whom they'd rather forget. The darkness brings them back.

Then there were the noises to deal with: the drips, the scratches, and the scurrying. This must be what happened when people were placed in sensory deprivation tanks.

As rehearsed, he waited for silence which soon rang in his ears. People had stopped talking, retreating alone into their minds, into the darkness residing inside all humans.

He heard footsteps behind him, no other groups were down here. He swallowed hard. He didn't know what it was. If it was a ghost, there would be an icy bite in the air.

The caves felt different today. The whole atmosphere felt agitated. Maybe he was imagining it.

He was supposed to count to 180, plunge his group in darkness for three minutes. Under his breath he reached fifteen when he felt watched. This was where he had seen that black mist. He tied to focus on giving a good tour but the more he was away from his group. The more he worried for their safety. What if, completely unaware, the mist had them surrounded?

He knew the way out. They didn't. Garth counted to 120. The air felt different. It was heavier, his breathing grew hoarse. He couldn't take it anymore.

There was an uneasy feeling around him that something bad was happening. He needed to get back to his tour group. He was wholly responsible for their safety.

Garth longed to see Cassie again. To make her smile at something he said.

He had planned on jumping out on them and shouting, "Boo!" That's what the other guides did, and it sent everyone hysterical.

All he needed to do was turn on his torch.

There was a chorus of shrieks. People dispersed from him in a human domino effect before gravitating back to the only source of light, his torch. Like the sun, they needed it. The relief was palpable when he handed back their kerosene lanterns. They held them that little bit tighter. Thankful to be brought out of their imposed solitary nightmares.

"That was bloody awful," one man admitted as he took back his lantern. Garth felt terrible, they had all felt *it*.

Afterwards, people followed him closely. They were quieter now more reflective, no one ever expected that to happen. Coming down here was a journey in more ways than they could imagine.

The rest of the tour went without a hitch. His group, who had been so eager to enter, were ecstatic to be out of the caves. He decided he'd earned himself a pint at the Bickley Arms pub next door to the caves when he took his lunch break.

There was relief in the air as people left, mostly heading to the cafeteria to get themselves a warm drink and a plate of sausages, chips, and beans. The coldness emanating from the caves could really get to you.

He lingered by the door accepting tips, not too bad for his first, no one guessing that he hadn't done this before. Secretly he waited for Cassie without making it too obvious.

He waited. Any second now she would emerge. He hoped she'd enjoyed herself. He couldn't wait to hear her thoughts, maybe she had questions to ask him about the caves. He was eager to ask her out properly.

A minute passed. Then two. Then three.

It was time to close the doors.

Eighteen people went into the caves. Only seventeen came out.

CHAPTER TWELVE

Cassie

Present Day: March 20th 10:30 a.m.

They had arrived at the Druids Altar. She didn't want to be here. Cassie stood away from the others. The altar pulled her close, but she refused to become its next offering.

This was the place where she felt *it* most. How could anyone not? She kept her eyes facing front towards the altar, avoiding the dark abyss with its swirling currents of dark air behind her

How could stone be worn so smooth like that? In the exact shape of a body? It must have taken hundreds, if not thousands, of years of victims being sacrificed on that slab to have made those indentations.

It was painful to stand over this grotesque murder scene. Thousands of innocent people murdered for the purpose of ritual magic.

She was clenching her teeth again. The time had come. She withdrew through the crowd of her tour group and waited on the periphery. The darkness touched her back as she faced away from it.

Cassie had been preparing herself for this moment, but it didn't make it any easier.

Garth took his position, holding his torch right in front of him, illuminating the altar's cold slab of stone, worn smooth through the centuries. He joked about human sacrifices taking place here, but it all made sense to Cassie. The laughter from the audience grew nervous.

Cassie looked away. She couldn't bear to look upon the altar any longer. In her mind she saw Hayley, tethered there for years, suffering the darkness that crawled under her skin and through her veins.

She remembered it clearly, this being the exact spot.

"Hey Cassie, when we're dead, lets come back and haunt this cave."

Was this where the darkness had first embraced her sister? Was she still captive? It was too late to save her. But Cassie could set her free.

She peered down the long tunnel, she was a mouse lost in a cave. It was strange that this was where Hayley had chosen to wander off, all those years ago.

Something beyond was watching her enrapt. They waited with bated breath to see if she would dare to enter the tunnel alone. Cassie recognized the presence; it was the same thing that kept watch on her when she was alone in their flat. She refused to be scared. Now she knew she hadn't been going mad. It was all real. Something was there beside her, calling out to her each night when the sun dropped.

It knew her.

Garth circled the group with a spring in his step. He had them all under his command. One by one he took away their lanterns, leaving them in darkness. "See you on the other side," he whispered to Cassie, brushing his hand with hers.

Plunged into a sea of black, so thick it felt like the smog that once plagued the Victorian streets of London, Cassie couldn't tell which way was up or down, left or right. She didn't know if she was firmly standing on the floor or being spirited away. But she had to do this. Her sister needed her help.

Her hands reached out to find solid rock but there was none to be found. The uncertainty was dizzying, she felt sick. She couldn't bear this, yet she must. For her sister's sake, for hers too.

If she remembered correctly, the tunnel was directly before her. Her legs felt like jelly, but she didn't have a choice. In the darkness there was nothing to see. Maybe it was better that way? Cassie took small steps away. Her beating heart felt like it was in her throat. People were too deep in their fears to notice her absence.

With each second, her resolve waned. Fighting against her rational nature to not drown in the darkness. Greeting her were flashes of white lightning too quick to comprehend the images being shown. It could have been a face. It could have been nothing. She heard whispers all around her in quiet echoes

She thought of Hayley, hoped she was close.

A breeze travelled down the long corridor she followed, carrying ancient heavy air recently disturbed.

Cassie only realized how far she'd walked when she heard screaming behind her followed by Garth's laughter. A dim light reminiscent of a fading sunset vanished in seconds.

Gath was all she wanted but it was too late. He disappeared before she could call out to him.

She was alone.

CHAPTER THIRTEEN

Bill

Present Day: March 20th, 12:00 p.m.

Bill set down his mug of tea on the counter of the visitor center. He'd finished checking the lanterns had enough kerosene to last the day. The coldness of the dark lingered on his skin.

Everything was as it should be, and the visitors were happy. The tours were going well. The café busy with the sound of cooking, the hissing of the coffee maker and the loud din of conversation.

After rolling a cigarette, Bill stepped outside to smoke. Sunlight filtering through the trees reached him. But he was still cold. He would always be cold.

Buds were appearing on trees. Winter was making way for Spring. Another turn of the year but still, the events of twenty-five years ago only felt like a yesterday away. Bill was a haunted man. He would never be free of his past.

All those years ago, he shook his head. That summer changed his life. He wished above all he could step back into the past. If only he could. Those memories made fresh once more by the new member of staff at the caves. Garth's arrival was both sweet and bitter inside his chest.

Bill had always kept Sandra close to him. This was more than a coincidence; this was an intervention of fate. Long ago, he fell into the curse of eternal optimism often suffered in youth. He had believed then there would have been many others afterwards to fill the void she left, but he had been wrong.

Returning from his cigarette break, he leaned against the countertop watching the steady stream of visitors filling up the empty pews, he only needed one side look at Garth, the new recruit, to know.

Time had slipped him by. Had it really been that long? The baby was now a young man, taller than him and broader too. Catching his own pale reflection in a picture frame, Bill saw what everyone else did. When did he get so old?

Once his towering 6ft 3 frame and broad shoulders had been intimidating, now people just saw an old man with a silver beard and thinning ponytail trailing down his sleeveless caves jacket. How long did he have left? Regret was mounting. There was bite in the old dog yet, but he looked back more than he could look forward.

In his heart he was still a biker rebel who spent his misspent youth driving around on his Harley. No one told him that one day, he'd start looking in the mirror and not recognize the old face staring back at him.

In a slightly different life, this new guy could have been his son. He would have loved a son like Garth but instead he had no son at all. He had no one.

Garth had no idea of their connection. As far as he was concerned, Bill was just another grumpy old tour guide. The oldest of the old guard.

Bill had to make sure Garth didn't last the week. He showed too much promise. It wouldn't be long until Fiona found out about him.

He couldn't be here.

Garth was weighed down with something heavy in his mind. Bill smiled to himself. Just like her son, Sandra was always a worrier, always wanted everyone to be happy, always putting the needs of others before her own.

It was proving difficult scaring him away from the caves. Garth had been acting strange since he first tour had finished. Now he was hunched over a table in the adjoining cafeteria. He wouldn't look anyone in the eye, he would rather be anywhere else. Garth was watching that locked door leading down to the caves, jumping at everything. Usually, first timers calmed down after they'd done their first tour. Not this one.

Bill looked at his watch, he was sat by himself on his lunch break nursing a cup of tea. With his good looks, he should have been down the pub with his mates, being chased by young women. Not sat alone as if it was his first day at school, on the verge of tears.

By all accounts, his first day at the caves was going well. His first tour group came out with big smiles, and he'd received a hefty tip. Bill had seen Garth stash a couple of notes into his back pocket. Even more reason to be down the pub which was next door. Why the hell was he drinking tea?

Normally, Bill didn't make much of an effort with the newer guides, not many could take the conditions. But Garth had gotten under his skin. After years of working for Fiona, he had forgotten that some people were kind. Usually, Bill waited until they proved themselves before he became friendly. He shouldn't have taken Garth under his wing. He should have scared him off much sooner. He had tried but the boy was tenacious.

Most people didn't last long here. Bill didn't blame them. *It* got to you after a while, being in the caves, all day long. It's a hard job, especially working for Fiona. Though it was only him unfortunate enough to have to directly deal with her. People often left quickly after their first week. Facing that darkness every day is harder than you think, hanging over everyone was a big responsibility leading people down there keeping them on the path, making sure they all stayed safe.

It was probably just a hangover of first day nerves lingering, but Bill felt an unexpected surge of tenderness for this young man. He walked over to Garth, calmly putting down his mug of strong brown tea marking out his territory. He would try his best to convince him to get a job elsewhere.

Never being one for words, Bill gave him a hearty pat on the back which caused Garth to jump bolt upright as if facing a judge and jury.

"Penny for them." Bill sat opposite and saw that up-close things were even worse. Garth was on the verge of tears. His eyes were swollen with red. Fingers shook as they busied themselves folding and unfolding a used sugar sachet. His nails were bitten right down. The clippings lay around him on the table.

"How did it go?" Bill added, to break the silence.

Garth looked to his left and right to see if anyone else was near enough to be within earshot.

He chose his words very carefully, saying it barely above a whisper, "I think I lost someone in the caves." He looked down and up waiting for the commotion.

Bill stayed very still.

"Impossible, someone would have noticed."

Garth shook his head. "She came on her own."

"On her own?" It wasn't usual to get a lone visitor; it was mostly American tourists who came here and local families.

"Eighteen went in, seventeen came out." Garth toyed with the torn sugar sachet. Crumpling and flattening it out over and over as if it were a ritual to summon back the missing person.

"When did you notice?"

Garth scratched his head giving his trembling fingers something to do. "It was when I made it dark for everyone, took away their lanterns, in the Druid section, right by the altar."

Bill cleared his throat and looked straight ahead. He didn't raise his voice, instead he nodded, closed his eyes. This could work out for the best. Garth wouldn't be working here much longer, and Bill wouldn't have to do a single thing. Poor boy. He didn't deserve this, but Bill had to protect him. It would be for his own good. Garth had no idea what the caves really were.

"Thanks for letting me know, I'll take a look."

So much for a quiet day at work.

CHAPTER FOURTEEN

Fiona

Present Day: March 20th, 12:15 p.m.

Today, *The Times* crossword puzzle would have to wait. It was hard to get stuck in with such a distraction. Fiona did not like distractions. There was not much she did like.

She ignored her coffee and stood with her hands on her aching hips, looking down at the scene in her home. There was a young maiden taking up her valuable time. She lay on the floor by Fiona's feet, bleeding out.

"Why me?" Fiona said. There was no end in sight. She had never asked for this role. But she had no choice—if she didn't carry out this task everyone would pay.

Despite the unfortunate but necessary head injury, the pulse remained. Sienna would still be useful, but it was more work for her to do.

This day had come round again. The preparations were endless. At least it was only once a year. Sienna needed to be moved back down to the cellar quarters before she came to. This one had a lot of bite.

Fiona shook her head. She had no idea from where she'd find the strength needed to carry her back down. She was still in pain from last night.

It hadn't been easy dragging Sienna unconscious into her car without anyone seeing. How on earth had she gotten this far?

Sienna shouldn't have woken up for hours. This needed dealing with before Fiona could do anything else. Nothing could go wrong, but the offerings so often fought against their fates. The grandfather clock standing sentry between the two arched windows chimed.

"The hour is nearly upon us."

Fiona kicked the woman's sprawled thigh. "All over my flooring as well," she muttered, noting the spray of blood stretching from wound to staircase.

Under different circumstances she would have insisted Sienna cleaned it. After all it was her mess, but it was better to move her before she had a chance to wake. Her house was too large and secluded for her to worry about neighbors, but she might try to escape again. Without disturbing the silence seeping up from the caves directly under her house just beyond the trees that sheltered the visitor center.

One of the tunnels fed directly into her house through the cellar. Fiona walked from the hallway down one of the passageways and into a secret room. She bowed her head as she approached her altar, dominated by a huge black mirror in an ornate silver frame looking out. It had been in her family for over a thousand years; built from the deepest rock of the caves, a link to the world down below. This mirror was different, it wasn't just for seeing what was over your shoulder.

Closing her eyes, she connected with the darkness inside of her, making the blessing of the five-pointed kiss with her right hand across her chest. She then opened her gaze and stared deeply into the mirror until she saw the pale face of a woman grown bitterly old. The White Lady. She was still sleeping, safely tucked away in her underground cavern but soon she would wake to feed. Fiona had popped down earlier to leave an offering of Sienna's jewelry.

If she didn't feed down there, she'd come up here in the dead of night. It was better this way. Fiona had a method when it came to choosing: each sacrifice, hand-picked after years of close observations. All her choices were those who deserved to spend eternity down there with Fiona's mistress.

The chosen girl was perfect. Fiona could feel her inner strength and her brightness. *A shame*, Fiona thought, *the girl had chosen to use it unwisely*. She could have achieved great things if she had not been so cruel to those unfortunate enough to cross paths with her. Even the girl's bones had power. Afterwards, they would be put to great use.

Each year of servitude took a higher toll. Fiona needed more and more to keep herself going. Fortunately, her mistress rewarded loyalty. She left the townsfolk alone. They needed each other, Fiona and The White Lady.

In the center of all her tools, was a knife with a shining black handle, always cold to touch. Fiona took it in her hand. From inside a large wooden box, she chose a wax-sealed vial, filling her syringe with dark liquid. She moved back to Sienna.

Fiona found a soft spot in the woman's neck and pushed on the syringe with a practiced hand. She counted to thirty.

Kneeling, she examined the woman. She was pleased. This one had very soft skin, not too plump, not too skinny just how her mistress liked them.

Her knees began to burn. It would be a struggle to stand up. Fiona couldn't help herself. She did something she had never done before. It wasn't allowed but each day, with her aging failing body, all she felt was pain. Her joints ached, her back ached, even her fingers. What she wanted was a little respite from the pain of living in an old body. It would help her prepare for the Spring Solstice. It would help everyone. Without pain she could easily carry out her work. The good people of Chislehurst would remain safe.

With her knife she took hold of the arm nearest to her and held it tight in her grip. She cut into the soft sweet flesh ever so slightly, her blade taking a fine ribbon of skin thin as a potato peeling. The temptation proved too great.

Fiona held the artwork in her hand up to the light. Sienna's skin was the color of spring blossom. She shouldn't be doing this, but as she held it in her hands the temptation grew. This was what her body wanted. She opened her mouth and in went the entire strip of skin.

She chewed and smiled, making noises of delight. Her taste buds found all the subtle notes of Sienna. Yes, this choice was particularly strong and powerful.

Her aches and pains resided. She felt strong again instead of defeated. Today would be a breeze without pain hindering her every move. Fiona had done well this year. Mistress would be pleased. She was not a woman easily impressed

Fiona wanted more, but it would be a great insult.

The phone rang as Fiona was about to grab hold of the woman's cold hands, splayed outwards like a bird in flight. She hesitated before answering. It could be something important. She had sent her *son* to the shops, and he was taking a long time. She hoped he wasn't having another episode. There was too much to do today.

"Hello?" she responded in a crisp voice used to deter idle chit chat.

"Fiona? It's me, Bill."

"Yes, what is it?"

"Look, the situation we're facing is this, a young woman has gone missing. Down in the caves. I've only just heard but I thought it best that you knew straight away."

Fiona pulled the phone cord tight around her fingers. "You must find this person before tomorrow morning." She considered after the initial shock. "We can't afford to let this get into the news. How could you lose someone like that? Really Bill?"

"It was the new guy, ma'am. It wouldn't have happened on my watch, but it has. I'm going to sort it. You don't need to take any action."

"What if the police order a search of the caves? This is most unsatisfactory."

"I'm going to look now; she disappeared by the altar."

Fiona hissed, "That is most unfortunate. Don't come back empty handed."

"Yes."

"Oh, and Bill, keep the new guy close to you, we may need to deal with him."

"No. Wait. Fiona? Let me handle this."

"Bill, you have until tomorrow morning and then I'm handling it."

Fiona put down the phone. Discretion was essential for their survival and for the town around them.

For centuries, the routine for the Order had been considerably easier. They'd been one big family, but as the ways of the world changed, her kind were wiped out. Whole families were persecuted in the name of religion.

Now it was just her.

People respected, even feared them before they slipped into the shadows of secret cults to survive. She would never be understood by the modern world that had built up around her.

Once the caves were surrounded by thick thorny forests that people were wise enough to avoid. Floating about in the taverns and on market days was many a tale of the forest being haunted, of ungodly creatures living there. Creatures no mortal should face.

People who knew the land left the area alone, gave it to the Druids to watch over, the wise men of the Celts.

For centuries there was calm.

Until Christianity ravaged the land.

People lost their old tales, and the old ways were forgotten. The forest became just another swathe of woodland that was eventually decimated into villages and towns. People got closer to the caves with each century.

Today, they lived right above them

Since they were first dug out, the caves were largely undisturbed. People knew not to go down there. Everything easily manageable until they were "rediscovered" at the turn of the twentieth century.

Now there were constant problems. Chislehurst was supposed to be a quiet leafy London suburb. The biggest complication faced in recent years was the caves having been turned into a tourist attraction after being a "safe" destination during the Blitz.

Fiona did all she could to stop it happening. But not even she could fight that tide. Everyone from cosplayers to rock bands to TV crews loved the caves. A playground for fun and misadventure but very few knew the truth, the real reason for that place coming into existence.

It wasn't an old mining network, but a nest.

Fiona still remembered the first time she met the White Lady. Her father had been an ambitious man and her mother loved the wealth that came from her husband. To win favor with the Druids they offered up Fiona, their only daughter. They walked her down to the Altar.

When the White lady approached partially hidden within a black mist, she took little Fiona down to the deepest reaches of her nest. Fiona never thought she would see daylight again. When the Druids died out, she made her way back up to serve as a loyal servant.

Time had taken its toll. A once beautiful woman is now a creature burrowed in blankets of darkness. An ancient forgotten goddess still living in parallel with the modern world. But still she must feed, always. She must be worshipped to prevent her creeping up the many hidden mine shafts leading directly into people's back gardens, decent people with children and loving homes. These were the people Fiona protected at all costs. She had dedicated her life to saving them. The White Lady had a whole city to feed upon, it was vital to make sure she stayed down there.

And then there were people like this woman, bleeding all over Fiona's house who deserved to be sacrificed. She made a mockery of everything humanity was trying to achieve.

As Fiona turned to gather up the chosen one, she got caught in the mirror. She dropped the young woman's arms, her limbs slapping against the floor with the sound of wet meat hauled up onto a butcher's block. Fiona stepped closer. A change had come about.

In the space of a few minutes, Fiona looked twenty years younger. But how? Her cheeks had risen, her wrinkles filled out. She could pass for sixty. Fiona couldn't believe it, she felt like herself again. For so long she had been the guardian of the caves she had forgotten how to live for herself.

All this from eating a tiny slither of human flesh? No, there must be something else. It was as if the caves had gotten in her blood. She was more powerful than she ever thought possible.

There was a young woman lost in the caves. An extra. She looked in the mirror again. Then at Sienna.

This one was hers.

Chapter Fifteen

Garth

Present Day: March 20th 5:00 p.m.

Nobody else noticed a brilliant young woman was missing, that was the worst part. For him it was as if a huge light had gone off. In this very moment, she was beneath his feet, lost and alone.

Cassie.

Like everyone else he had to carry on. Pretending that she was up here with him and not down there and alone. Bill had told him to act as if nothing had happened, don't tell anyone, and not to worry because he would sort it. Garth trusted Bill. He did as he was told even though he didn't think it was right. Garth was a traitor and even worse, a coward.

"It's my fault," he kept whispering to himself. He had led a young woman straight into danger. He'd left her in the dark. She was alone. It was all his fault.

His first day nerves had been fraught. He'd worried about forgetting his lines, leaving his tour group bored instead of fascinated. He never thought to worry about losing someone down there in the fold of darkness.

Garth kept hoping each time he took a group through the caves that she would just reappear at the Druid's Altar and follow him out into the light of day, but she never did. The darkness had swallowed her whole and left no trace nor trail. But Bill said he'd take care of it.

As he stomped through dark tunnels with his lantern shining the way, Garth re-lived every second he had spent with her down there. How could he have known then that those would be his only moments with her?

The romance of his life could be played from beginning to end within one hour. He fought to hold back tears when he got to the altar and felt no joy in terrifying the visitors when he jumped out on them in the pitch black. They screamed, causing the caves to moan in response and one man kicked him in the shin with his walking boot. That he deserved. He'd never felt so bad in his entire life.

First day on his new job. He had messed up. He dreaded going home and having this conversation with his mum.

Not even she could spin this into something positive. But his worries were so trivial against what Cassie must be going through right now. She may never get to go home again.

Would they let him go? If they didn't let him come back, how would he be able to look for Cassie?

The life he had always dreamed for was about to be taken from him. The gap between his dream life and his real life frightened him.

All those years he'd spent dreaming of the day when he would be allowed to explore down there in the subterranean caves unhindered, completely by himself, going to all the forbidden places sealed off to the public. To know every secret that remained. He'd always fantasized of finding buried treasure, long lost secrets of the Druids. He never wanted to go down there again.

The caves weren't the same anymore, he felt scared knowing the things he did. Soon it would be a graveyard. Her bones might never be found if something wasn't done.

He wanted to be away from here, but the place kept him tethered.

As an introvert too sensitive for the wider world, Garth had never really been able to make friends, but it was okay. A background person, he was happier in his own head but still he pined for the day when he would find his soulmate. With Cassie he'd felt a real connection growing between them. He'd never had that with anyone but his mum.

Cassie had been everything that he was searching for. It had taken him years to meet someone like her. Would he ever get the chance again?

Navigating fate and destiny was a tricky thing. He'd always been shy, choosing to hide in his room when his friends were out getting drunk and talking to girls. He never did well at school, he couldn't even be a proper geek.

Had Cassie felt it too? She might have been his one and only, had he not let her go.

Of all the places to lose someone.

And where was she? How long could she survive for? He hated thinking of her, lost, alone and afraid, struggling with tears in her eyes, unable to feel which way was up and down with that unnatural darkness closing in around her like a fist, blaming him.

Garth had taken her lantern away, she had nothing. Even by now, after a few hours she would be going mad with the hallucinations which quickly set in when there was nothing for the eyes to hold on to.

Down there was a darkness unlike any other.

All the old boys who worked here had warned him of that. That's why you always brought two torches with you. One for your hands and one as back-up. A third if it was particularly strong that day. Your sanity depended on it.

There were things down there that like to play games with you. Garth had felt it too. When you're all alone in the darkness, your worst fears came forward taking advantage.

There was no escape from the darkness down there.

He saw Bill alone in the office, preparing to go on a solo mission, bringing eight torches, food and drink and a medical kit. He'd been so good about it considering the implications, which made it worse. Garth didn't deserve any kindness. "Bill, please. Let me come down and look for her. I know I can find her."

"No," Bill wouldn't even discuss it.

"Please. I can do this." Garth took a step closer.

"I've said no Garth. Do as you're told."

"Why can't I come?"

Bill sighed. "It's got to be done quickly. I can't risk attracting attention."

"But it's my fault. I'm the one in trouble."

"Close your door on the way out."

Garth knew Bill was hiding something. But he had every faith that if anyone could find Cassie it would be him. He made himself a cup of tea. Bill was just trying to protect Garth, he just wanted to find Cassie before he had to alert management. He was simply trying to save Garth's job.

Garth truly had no idea what he'd done to that poor girl.

Bill said time and time again he would deal with it. He made Garth promise not to call the police. The media would get involved and who knows what they would stir up. He said Garth would go to prison if anyone else found out.

The caves would be ruined, Bill forewarned. Garth was careful not to press too hard in a very difficult and fraught situation, but he noticed there was something else bothering Bill, something much more pressing. His tones were growing ever curter and more clipped. He was battling with something inside.

To a trained eye it would look as if Bill was scared.

"Please let me come with you," Garth said one last time.

"No."

"I'll come back tomorrow," Garth promised, "when the caves are shut for maintenance."

Bill spun around, taking Garth by the shoulders, and pushed him out of the small windowless office. He stayed still after falling to the floor. Bill's stance painfully reminded him of his father.

"Never come back here. Get on a plane and never come back. Stay away, boy." Finding Cassie was more important than keeping his job and staying on Bill's good side. He had to find Cassie. With or without Bill's permission.

Chapter Sixteen

Sienna

Present Day: March 20th, 1:33 p.m.

"What?" she hissed.

How had this happened? Again? She had made it out of the cage, out of the cellar. She had been so close to the front door illuminated with sunshine. She was reaching for the telephone. She was about to call Rhys for help.

But now Sienna was back in the wicker cage. Trapped. Back where she started. Once again in this forgotten room drenched in the tang of rotting soil. The back of her head cold, wet and pulsating with pain. She'd been hit hard. A headache blurred her vision. Someone really didn't like her today.

Who had moved her back down here? For now, she was alone, but just how many nutjobs was she dealing with?

If only she had some paracetamol for her thumping headache, however she realized the pain was good, it fueled her anger.

Anger would be the only thing keeping her alive today. She noticed as she sat up that her left arm had been bandaged. She raised it and winced, had someone taken a big chunk out of her?

The door opened.

"Who's there?" Sienna shuffled along, brought her right eye up close to her cage.

There was a tiny gap allowing her to see. Wan candlelight illuminated the table stacked by the wall.

The elderly woman whom she'd met in the hallway from before walked in and closed the door behind her.

Instincts screamed not to trust that old woman. Not anymore. There was something different about her. How could she be the same sweet old lady she saw earlier? She was no longer frail and stooping, she'd become stronger, more upright. Her hunting instincts fully engaged.

Sienna watched on. This old woman was unnatural. Her skin was too clear for someone her age. Her eyes were as bright and curious as a child's. A force of dark energy coursed through her veins.

It was the woman from the bar. Sienna remembered now. A strange old woman had been watching her closely. Never once did she take her eyes off Sienna that night. At the bar she tried to talk to Sienna when she stood close to her, but Sienna had quickly walked away. Why had she targeted Sienna like this? It just didn't make any sense.

Wiping away silent tears of frustration, Sienna tried to sit up. She could recognize her own kind. This woman had a menace about her. She was in deep trouble.

It was clinical the manner she worked, selecting various bottles from the shelves above the worktable.

There was a heavy looking pestle and mortar which she used without struggle to grind dried herbs. For this old woman, there was nothing out of the ordinary to have a young woman trapped in her cellar.

Sienna didn't get fooled often. Had she finally met her equal? This woman was a true bitch, a female powerhouse. *Being in total control, honey.* A woman used to fighting titans and winning, advancing her position with every battle.

But she wasn't going to win with Sienna.

"I see you are awake." The old woman didn't turn. She even had eyes in the back of her head.

"Who are you?" Sienna leant in, curling her fingers into fists baying for blood.

"Fiona, dear," she replied curtly. She went back to the door and called out, "It's time."

With the light on, Sienna saw that the cellar she was in had been converted into hideous living quarters. The walls dripped with green damp, glistened with it. The furniture sparse, a wooden workbench pushed up to the wall and a long table that could be used as a bed. She would not be sleeping here.

In the corner there was a chipped white Victorian clawfoot bath, a wooden workbench lined up against the wall in front of her, chaotic with tools and bottles. The floor was rock, the foundations of the land straight from Mother Earth.

"Where am I?"

"It's not about where you are, but where you're going, young lady," Fiona said with a wink.

A younger man in his fifties entered the room with a bowed head. He smiled revealing all his teeth of a variety of angles.

"Don't get attached, she won't be with us for long." Fiona appeared to be having a private joke with herself.

He'd been told not to look at her. *Who was this guy?* Sienna wondered. His skin was so sickly, podgy like a baby, had he ever been allowed outside? He looked like an opportunity.

Fiona wouldn't fall under the spell of manipulation, she had been born from cold hard iron, but this man might be able to unwittingly help Sienna escape.

As a young woman she'd experienced worse than him. He was bound to be meek and pliable. Maybe just a glance of her body would be enough to set her free.

She would do anything to get out of here. Anything. Had she gotten herself caught up in a human trafficking network? This woman didn't seem the type, but money is money. Everyone had a price.

Her cage was opened. A rush of cold stagnant air came in. In other situations, she would be feeling sick from it, but in this room, she was grateful not to be taunted by the stench of human filth from the cage.

Sienna backed away, but it was barely big enough to hold her. There was no shelter to be found. Nowhere to retreat where she could feel safe. Strong arms reached in and grabbed hold of her grubby, trembling, and useless legs. Unable to kick they submitted to violent muscle cramps when the old lady grabbed her ankles. She had great power. Stronger than the man, she hauled her out with expert ease and kept hold of her arms and legs. Earlier she had been a frail old woman but now she looked different, younger. Fiona was getting stronger as Sienna was getting weaker. She looked at the bandage on her arm. What was Fiona doing to her?

Together the old woman and her manservant carried her over to the wooden table without speaking and laid her down, stretching out her limbs, taking them out of her control. This duo had done this before, many times. Before she had time to notice, her hands and feet were bound with something cold and biting.

"Get off me now."

The man stroked Sienna's arm making her his pet. Fiona pushed him aside to continue working. She ripped away Sienna's tights in seconds. Then she took the hem of Sienna's most expensive dress and began to snip with cold metal.

"No!"

The fabric quickly gave way.

"What are you doing?"

Sienna closed her eyes and screamed. They didn't stop. The noise didn't bother them or impede on their business. The coldness of the cellar found all of her skin.

They took away all her clothes, cutting them into scraps that were quickly swept away. She was going to have to escape naked. But she'd do it. She'd do anything now.

Next came cold wet rough scraps of cloth grinding against her skin. They washed her red raw but what for? Was she to be a living doll? She'd heard tales of women being kept in basements made to bear child after child. She shivered. How could it have come to this? She told herself over and over, this wasn't really happening to her. This wasn't her body being prepared by candlelight bathing her skin. The tincture was applied to her skin, it smelt of rosemary. All around her was Fiona's voice, alight with a song composed of an old long-lost language. A song which grew with power as her unwavering voice rose, the sound curdled around her.

I'm somewhere else.

CHAPTER SEVENTEEN

Bill

Present Day: March 20th, 4:20 p.m.

He would never get a break. He was trapped here and now he was dragging Garth down with him. He'd tried so hard to scare him off make his training as dangerous as he could, but Garth kept coming back.

The situation beneath in the caves was messy. Fiona had sworn him to secrecy but Jenny the manager had overheard Bill and Garth arguing. She also knew there was someone missing.

Jenny was a good woman. A young, widowed mother of two, she didn't deserve to be involved in this. The responsibility of cleaning it up always stopped with Bill. He was the go-to dependable, solid as a rock, afraid of nothing type of guy who could deal with anything. A victim of his own efficiency to take care of things. More suited to the marines than working as a tour guide.

No matter the outcome he was going to have to tell Jenny the woman had been found and pray that Fiona wouldn't find out that Jenny knew anything about this. He vowed to clean up this mess. Only one person needed to die today.

Bill had never wanted to be the guy who took care of everything Had never asked for the burden of being the one to venture beneath the ground and get the girl whom Garth managed to lose on his very first tour.

The folly of youth never failed to surprise him. Bill had done some stupid things in his life, but he'd never been stupid enough to go down there at this time of year. The caves were closed every year on 21st March for good reason. He checked his watch; he didn't have long.

It brought back life-wrenching memories, particularly at this time of the year at the Spring Equinox when the darkness of the world was forced to make a retreat, though not without taking a bite.

He should have let Garth deal with the aftermath of the mess he had created. Except Bill knew what that would involve. He was only a boy. Garth didn't know anything at all other than suffering. For the first time in years, Bill had warmed to another person, *her* son.

He couldn't let Garth have that fate.

Garth had said she was a young woman. It wouldn't be long until she would be missed. Cassie would have many friends and family who'd notice her gone. The prefect poster girl for a missing woman. The police would be called, and her face would be everywhere.

To find Cassie, or discover what happened to her, there would be a public appeal and extensive search. The police might find her on the CCTV watching the streets of London. Those cameras could show her walking to Chislehurst Caves but never coming out of them.

It would draw attention to the cave. The police and outside world would never understand. Their attention would get him and the rest of the local population into a lot of trouble.

He packed his supplies into his rucksack. There was no other person in the office with Bill, yet he knew he wasn't alone.

In the absence of a breeze, the solitary lightbulb hanging from a cord swayed in the gloom. Fiona had done a complete U-turn on their situation. She'd ordered Bill to leave Cassie there, she was very adamant about that. But she wasn't the chosen one. Fiona was up to something, and it never bode well to go against her wishes.

But he had to do this for Sandra. He owed her.

Something was behind him, a presence too still to be breathing. It was one of *them*. The air dropped in temperature. His bones ached with cold. He slightly turned his shoulder to look and saw a shape coming up behind him. Dead eyes boring into the back of his head pummeling like pneumatic drills.

Still, he's never been able to get used to their gaze full of sorrow. Imploring to anyone who can see them for a better existence. He's spent years researching occult matters, but he was still unable to grant them the peace they deserve. He doubted whether he ever could. For the unlucky few, death never ends.

"Have you seen a young woman down there?" Bill whispered, barely audible against the humming of the solitary light bulb hanging above him.

No answer.

Bill reluctantly turned to face the guest. A miner dressed in grubby threadbare clothes stood in front of him, still holding his pickaxe in his white dusty hands ready for work.

In life this man would have been formidable, strong with wide shoulders and a brooding scowl. As a ghost he was pressed up against the walls, fearful.

The ghost shook his head. Bill turned back around, when he reached the door, the thing was gone. He heaved with relief, for now. The older he got the more he disliked death.

A flashlight in each hand poised and ready, he entered the caves.

It was a different atmosphere entirely when you're there alone. When there was nothing to distract you from the silence weaving its web around you. Pulling you under without you being aware of its drag. Down here silence had a pulse, sentient, aware. Always hungry.

A fact that a tour guide would never impart was that in certain areas it was impossible to make an echo even from a scream. The sound was immediately swallowed by something unseen, a pulse that devoured all living matter, even sound.

Bill was ever cautious. He kept his breathing quiet and controlled, his footsteps light and springy. There was no joy down here, only waiting. If death was a realm you could visit, this would be it.

His hiking boots scuffled the dirt into small clouds behind him as he passed the old Second World War office that stood empty. From inside the office, the fading garishly painted mannequins of Mr. Collins and Mrs. Cooper still poised with the register, stared at him with their hollow eyes.

"Mr. Collins, Mrs. Cooper," he bowed his head in acknowledgement.

It appeared to Bill that Mrs. Cooper moved slightly to sneer at him. Even in the light, this place was playing tricks on him.

The office, small and squat, was now a tourist attraction. Once he'd had to go in there to do repairs and it became so cold his bones ached for days afterwards.

Something bad happened in that little building, something that still lingered. People thought it quaint but during World War Two it was a gateway.

If you were allowed sanctuary in the caves, you were safe from the German bombing raids that churned up London's streets into heaps of blood, rubble, and bone. If not, you had to go back up to the surface and pray for the morning to come and the bombs to cease dropping.

These caves had provided shelter to 15,000 Londoners. Each night they would gather and descend deep in these caves. Piling up in rows and rows of bunk beds littered along the tunnels and passageways.

Listening to the sounds of war above, they would lay in the darkness hoping their homes would still be standing when they re-emerged in the morning.

Some people came here because they no longer had anywhere to live, the caves became their home. It was a desperate time, people had to do what they could to survive. Even coming down here night after night.

Bill didn't linger. How could Garth have been so stupid to lose someone on his first tour? Not in all his twenty-five years as a tour guide had he ever heard of visitors accidentally getting lost. No one was stupid enough to wander off. It was a tale they told to the parents to make sure they held on to their children.

Garth was in bits, rightly so. Even his shoulders sagged with the guilt of what he had caused for that young girl. He was a sensitive soul who felt everything too deeply for too long. He would never forgive himself if she wasn't found and it was a big *if* down there.

At least this meant he wouldn't last here much longer as a tour guide. It was for the best. Once sacked, Garth would be free to live a normal life, unlike the one Bill's been made to endure.

His knees groaned as they navigated across the uneven stone floor. He should be tinkering with his Harley listening to his favorite blues records whilst planning out his next cross-county route.

There were only a few hours in which Bill could save this missing girl and get out—if saving was still an option. Fiona would soon find out he'd gone against her orders. She saw everything down here. There was a niggling doubt in his head that this mess hadn't been caused by Garth's colossal stupidity.

CHAPTER EIGHTEEN

Bill

Present Day: 20th March, 4:45 p.m.

As soon as he discovered rock'n'roll, Bill had always wanted to go to the States. It was his dream as a young man to ride across the American highways on his bike, drinking in dive bars, staying at crappy roadside motels with the sun behind him. All that wide-open space. All that Californian sunlight. He'd saved up, enough for the trip of a lifetime. He wanted to buy a one-way ticket and never return to the scudding grey skies of England.

That all became a distant dream when Fiona took him down one day into the caves. He'd only meant to work at the caves for the summer. Nothing more than a stop gap. Every penny earned was going to be a cent for the U.S. But there were qualities in him Fiona had taken a shine to. It had been his downfall. She brought him here alone. The caves were closed for maintenance, which always fell on 21st March, the Spring Solstice.

Fiona had asked for him to take the night watch. She wanted to ensure nobody got in, but it was a difficult job. These caves attracted the weirdos, before he'd caught goth kids trying to worship, their presence betrayed with candles and incense. It was Bill's job to patrol at night. He wasn't the only one who knew where all the secret entrances and exits were.

During his years on the night watch he'd stumbled across loners wanting to commune with the spirits. Witches came in their covens at the turns of the year, even partygoers trying to start a moonlight rave as was the fashion in the '90s before it was shut down. They wouldn't if they really knew what was down there.

The truth had never sat easy with Bill.

He'd seen a lot during his years here, but he always kept his head down and his mouth shut but his eyes still took it all in. This place was never a mine, that was never its true purpose.

Fiona had tricked Bill, she was kind to him only up to the point where she brought him to the altar. On that day the altar had been prepared, there was man tied up. Had he not had tape over his mouth he would have been screaming for his life. His limbs thrashed eye wide with fear following something behind Bill shoulder.

There were approaching footsteps. Slowly a figure took shape out of a black mist. A woman walking towards them. She had lived down here so long she had become one with the caves, each tunnel, each crevice, and shadow under her command.

It was like watching a horror movie where a creature made of malice emerges from their hiding spot to prey on their chosen victim. Except he wasn't behind the safety of a television screen. It was real and he was in it.

Bill tired his best to free the man, but the chains held him tight. Effortlessly the approaching woman pushed him away. He hit a wall with the breath knocked out of him.

The White Lady was not interested in Bill, she only had eyes for the man tied to her altar. She feasted on that man in the same way a young man feasts on a kebab after downing ten pints at his local. She showed no mercy, no restraint.

She took his heart straight from his chest. It lay open as she ate it in one. Bill watched the man shudder towards death. It was already too late to save him. She ripped him open, with the ease of a child tearing open a Christmas present from under the tree. The altar became red, everywhere he looked was the viscera and goop that had once formed a man. Now it was a mess. It made Bill feel very fragile.

Bill knew he would be next, but he couldn't muster the strength to move. His body racked with fright refused to move. His brain had shut down. He knew what was coming but his mind was refusing to tell him.

Instead, when the man was nothing more than glistening white bones sucked clean of their blood and marrow, she clambered down.

After eating she appeared much younger. Once she had been a strange kind of beautiful with black eyes and moonshine skin. She walked towards him smiling with the satisfaction of a purring cat and disappeared back down the long tunnel used by the druids.

"What have you done Fiona?" Bill struggled to get his breath back. "You tricked me."

"We've all been tricked, Bill. It's over now for another year."

"I'm handing in my resignation in the morning. Find another fool to do your dirty work."

"Oh Bill, if only it were that simple."

Fiona straightened her jacket and promptly left, following the route leading back to the outside world.

Bill followed vowing to never return. He rubbed his right cheek; something had scratched him. Why had Fiona brought him here? The White Lady should have killed him but instead she did something much worse.

She had been human, until the caves had chosen her, and she had chosen Bill. All it had taken was a scratch upon his skin to condemn him. The White Lady had drawn his blood and tasted it and that was enough to keep him forever. There was no antidote to the Old Ones and their magic

Fiona had decided Bill could be of use. There was no getting away from the caves. Bill would remain here. He would never see a Californian sunset, never feel the breeze of the Pacific Ocean. He would never set foot in a dive bar. She needed eyes and ears on the place, from that day the role went to him. What was Bill's crime? Why had she chosen him?

He never trusted anyone again after that.

The scar on his cheek still burned from where the White Lady had struck him.

Maybe this girl was another weirdo, but even so, she needed to be found.

This girl, Cassie, could still be alive, but she wouldn't last long. Tomorrow was the Spring Solstice, soon the White Lady would come looking for her offering. What if she found Cassie instead?

Maybe Cassie could find her way out in time but there was little chance of escape if she didn't have a torch with her. Never mind food and water. They came second in priority to light.

That darkness was alive, teeming. These caves were never ending. Always looping back on themselves. The possibilities for getting lost were endless.

His waterproof jacket brushed against the lining of the caves, unleashing a fresh wave of malevolence The reason that houses became haunted over time was because certain materials such as rock and particularly bricks absorbed energies, particularly negative energies of hate and evil. It was especially true down here.

Underneath his feet, the floor resembled a hardened beach of sand made frozen from the absence of light. He wished there were noise. The silence became deafening, confused his other senses. How could silence feel so loud? This place was soaked in death.

Bill stopped at the end of one tunnel and raised his torch to view the many smaller offshoots. Tunnels wide as gaping mouths opening to sift and take its fill. Mouths that never ended eventually leading down to wide bellies and narrow bowels.

To stay alive, it was best to stick to the wider tunnels, the smaller ones had a devastating tendency to wind around like a coiled snake chasing its own tail. To get lost in one would cause nausea and confusion.

Bill must be practical. Garth said she came here alone.

Would any of the other tour group have remembered her? Would the police be able to trace them to ask? There were no records kept detailing visitors' names and numbers. No proof of her coming here if she paid for her ticket with cash.

Nobody counted on the door. It was never that busy during the week.

It would take nothing to cover up the fact she was ever here.

CHAPTER NINETEEN

Fiona

Present Day: March 20th, 5:05 p.m.

Each year Fiona found it easier to pick an offering for her mistress, but this was the first year that someone had gone down of their own accord. On Fiona's strict orders, no one was to go looking for Cassie. She would not tolerate mutiny in her caves. Anyone who disobeyed would be severely dealt with. They would be introduced to the White Lady for an encounter they'd never forget.

For years she's brought people down hoping to replace herself, but the White Lady had never taken a liking to anyone except for Fiona. She simply ate those Fiona brought down. Once she sees you, she keeps you. It only takes a scratch to be bound to her.

Now there was hope. Fiona would keep Sienna for herself. A prize righteously earned after a lifetime of loyal service to the White Lady. Sienna might last for months if Fiona took only the skin before delving into the organs. Fiona wondered which pieces would be the most bountiful. How much mortal flesh would she need to look twenty-five again? After tomorrow, once her mistress had fed and returned to her domain for another year, Fiona would find out. No one was going to miss a woman of Sienna's caliber.

Her black scrying mirror saw all the darkness of the world, the deeds people committed. The most heinous usually escaped the law, but nothing remained hidden in the darkness her mistress controlled. Fiona had made it her life's work to seek them out.

Fiona stood in front of her mirror, wanting to see Sienna's life play for her one last time before it was erased along with her existence.

These are the people Fiona hated the most, those who are free from everything that binds others, free from guilt, shame, duty, fear, and lack of imagination.

Fiona saw her reflection. The restorative effects of eating a slice of Sienna had already worn off. Her cheeks and eyes had sunk back down. Carrying Sienna back down to the cellar hadn't been easy.

Life was cruel, Fiona had been allowed to live for centuries but had aged as fast as any mortal and now she endured without end in the body of an old, withered woman.

Eventually she would die but her soul would live on enduring within a rotting carcass. What then?

Mortals longed for endless youth and vitality as she had once done. She felt she had spent all her life being old.

Life could have been much different if she had always looked young, had been allowed to live beyond the boundaries set out for her. All these years and she had never left London.

She barely remembered being a child. Fiona's father was a wealthy merchant. Her parents had grand ambitions for their two sons, but Fiona was largely left alone. She had been a pretty child and they knew it would be easy to marry her off.

If they had taken the time to get to know her, they would have realized she possessed unique talents. Others called it *The Gift*. When a pestilence arrived at their village her ointments kept it bay. News spread amongst the peasants, and it was Fiona not the Druids that they turned to for help and guidance.

The order of the Druids held all the power and soon saw her as a threat. Her father was keen to trade with them. Londinium nearby was booming, and the Roman Army was in dire need of chalk and flint which the cave possessed in great quantities. It wouldn't anger the White Lady if only a little was taken from the top layers and she was given her pick of miners to feast upon.

Her childhood was over quickly once her father had offered up his daughter to the Druids in return for mining rights. The Druids offered her up as sacrifice but when Fiona saw the White Lady approaching, she fought back. The flames they held re-ignited under her command forcing the White Lady back.

Instead of being angered, the White Lady was impressed. The chains were loosened, and Fiona was taken down deeper than anyone had ever been before. The White Lady taught Fiona how to read, she was given free rein to read all her books, cast spells and learn the secrets of magic that the Druids had been so keen to learn from the ancient Celts before them.

Everyone she had known and loved was buried in the churchyard. Christianity had swept over the land and people denounced their old gods. The White Lady needed help to survive, Fiona was allowed back up from the caves, given everything she had ever wanted except a life of her own. The only person who kept her going was her son, he too had been given the gift of an unnaturally long life.

One year she tried to escape from the caves, she has never forgiven herself for what the White Lady did out of revenge.

Her only solace in life was choosing the degenerates for the White Lady. The White Lady had chosen Fiona, and Fiona had chosen Sienna.

Once the White Lady saw you, she kept you. Sienna was strong willed and venomous, but she didn't stand a chance of survival.

Tomorrow, Fiona had the chance to be young again. She wanted to have fun, live carefree and see what the modern world had to offer her.

Chapter Twenty

Bill

Present Day: 20th March, 5:30 p.m.

Garth had no idea what had gone on between Bill and his mother, Sandra. He may never know. There was so much in this world and beyond that boy was yet to understand.

It was many years ago when life had seemed perfect to Bill. In his golden years he was endlessly brimming with the eternal optimism that often blinds the young, making fools of them all before they reach twenty-five. How could Bill have known then what the future was going to do to him.

It had happened before Garth was born. It had been the real thing that only happens once if you're lucky. Their love, so sudden and complete like heaving ripe fruit hanging from a tree, too soon, too much, it burst open and rotted before it hit the ground.

Bill had been an idiot not to realize the true worth of what they had. It was a likely ending. Scared by his feelings for her, he'd played about. Sandra quickly met someone else. On the rebound she fell pregnant, and, in those days, Sandra had no other option but to marry her second choice. She forgot Bill, her first love. Nine months later she had a little boy, called him Garth.

Bill had always thought of her through the years. It was impossible not to. She always looked lovely whilst walking her little boy in the park. When Sandra smiled as she pushed her son on the swings, she almost looked happy, if not for that haunted look in her eyes. Age never stamped its mark on her beauty.

Bill never said hello, wouldn't allow himself to get close enough for her to spot him. She never knew he was there at all. After their affair he withdrew from the world. People assumed he had moved away. To look upon her was to feel that pain of their severance freshly cut. Losing Sandra had been worse than losing a limb.

Although Sandra had quickly forgotten about him when she entered motherhood. Garth was everything to her. She never came looking for him after they had parted. He thought that was to be his eternal punishment, to always be looking in the rosy glow of her life from the coldness outside.

He had been wrong.

The caves felt colder this time. Or maybe it was him. How different life could have been for him, for the both of them if he hadn't been so stupid in his youth. The golden period of life which feels like it lasts for only a few minutes, but the choices made last for a lifetime.

It was Sandra who was made to bear the brunt of suffering Bill's stupid mistake. Why must women suffer the folly of Man? Eternally cursed to be born as vessels of pain and suffering.

Not long after the wedding, her new husband had found out about Bill. When he placed his ring around her finger, he had assumed she was innocent and unblemished. He soon saw the truth that he could never quite replace Bill.

When Garth was born, Bill often saw her at the park. Bruises appeared on Sandra. At first, a lone accidental cloud of hurt appeared on her arm. Then came regular clusters of mottled green, yellow, and purple. Cheeks became swollen, too tender to touch under carefully applied make-up. She tended to fall over a lot on a Friday night after her husband arrived home from the pub.

But what could Bill have done? Could he have changed his history and hers?

She'd made it clear she didn't love him after his mistakes. He didn't deserve her forgiveness.

He could have been that shoulder to cry on. He lived on the mercy of hope that one day she would leave her husband. It killed him each day to know she couldn't. She wasn't the sort of mother to upset her son. She would be bound to him till the day she passed.

Bill couldn't leave he was bound to the caves. He couldn't have taken her to safety, to a new life.

The husband got worse; Bill rarely saw her about town. He hadn't seen her for years, once or twice he thought she might have moved away. She left no trace except the pain in his heart. He'd never stopped thinking of her.

In a narrow tunnel he came to an abrupt stop and clutched his chest. Waited a few moments for the striking pain to recede. He was completely alone. It was doing him no good thinking of her, especially down here. His heart wasn't what it once was.

Still, he had their picture by his bedside table, creased and peeling at the edges. She was leaning in to kiss him as he posed in the photo booth. Her long blonde hair often tickled his neck when she leaned in for a kiss. He'd kept, as a memento, the old ticket stubs of the bands they saw down in the caves securely tucked in his wallet.

He didn't do a single thing and the shame haunted him, but he would do something now.

Chapter Twenty-One

Bill

Present Day: March 20th, 6:00 p.m.

Now, Garth worked at the caves. He was in danger.

When Garth turned up that morning for his first day of training, he had his mother's eyes. It had to be him, that little boy Bill used to see from time to time. The only person on this earth who could make his mother smile. Bill knew for sure from the surname when he saw it on the roster.

Bill got chatting to him, wanting to know if his mother was still about, still alive, and well.

"Do you still live at home? Are things alright with your mum and dad?" Bill grew worried, wishing he'd never probed when Garth grew uneasy.

"Just me and Mum now."

"Oh?" Had there been a divorce? Was Sandra finally free to love and live again?

"My dad died about six months ago."

"Sorry to hear that." But Bill wasn't sorry and from the way Garth looked, with no hint of sadness in his eyes, no grief weighing him down, he wasn't sorry either. Bill didn't need the details. He knew Sandra was coping well.

It wasn't easy for Garth to talk about his father's recent death. From the dark gleam in Garth's eyes Bill knew he was glad his father was dead.

Bill decided there and then that enough was enough. After this was all sorted, he was going to pay her a visit.

Would flowers and chocolate be inappropriate? Paltry and meagre against their history. A long honest chat was what was needed. He just hoped she would answer the door to him. But first he had to find Cassie and get out of here. He just needed Sandra to know it had always been her. He'd never married. Never met anyone else. There wasn't space in his heart for another woman.

Movement in the cave sounded behind him. His second metal flashlight searched the ceiling above his head.

It became a weapon.

Bill relaxed his stance slightly after hearing children's laughter, little legs running through the endless tunnels. Playing their war time games of hide-and-seek.

It wasn't the noisy ghosts that scared him, it was the silent stalking White Lady.

He headed first to the Druid's Altar; this was where Garth said Cassie had disappeared. He looked around. It seemed too much of a coincidence.

Was the White Lady getting too greedy? They couldn't allow cave visitors to be snatched in the darkness. But no one could control the White Lady. If she was preying on the tourists, the secret would soon get out.

He shone his torch along the long Druid tunnel, once the site of arcane rituals. There was no way he was going down there. The light in that particular spot would only barely penetrate the darkness. Bill looked closer, his torchlight seemed to shiver and retreat against the forces of darkness.

Unable to look down into the tunnel for long, he shone the torch back on the cave floor. No signs of a blood trail or uneaten flesh. The altar was still clean and undisturbed. No marks of something heavy like Cassie being dragged along the floor against her will. He came to the uneasy conclusion that Cassie had walked away willingly, but even though he was now standing in the same spot where she was last seen, he was no closer to knowing why.

Even if you didn't know the truth of the caves, you still wouldn't want to go down that tunnel. Gut instincts were what kept you alive down here. Unless the darkness had found a way to get to you and draw you in.

Was the White Lady getting stronger?

He thought of Garth and Sandra. If he could help them, he would. Shining his light down the tunnel, the coalescence of shadows immediately retreated as if burnt. His bones urged him to run.

But this was something he had to do.

He edged back to the altar and checked again his supplies in the rucksack. Eight torches and three packs of batteries. Extra strength batteries.

Bill wasn't taking any chances. He wasn't going to die today. Not until he had made things right with Sandra. His first and only love. He couldn't die without telling her his truth.

She could take back his immunity to her at any time. The only thing he had looked forward to in life was dying in the comfort of his own bed within the sanctuary of a sweet dream, not from having his heart ripped out and eaten.

There was a time when *this* was common knowledge, Fiona had told him. Not long after getting scratched from the White Lady he became privy to the real nature of the caves.

Fiona wanted him to help select offerings. She had said it was simple as choosing a cut of meat from the butchers, but he wouldn't be a part of that.

"Bill, the service I provide is essential," she'd said over a cup of black coffee. "Long ago, the local people knew what went on down here. What had to take place each year. They had accepted this fact as they did the inevitability of their own deaths. They understood. It kept the settlement above in order, no one stepped out of line."

But in these more modern times, people lost their understanding of the old ways, of The White Lady who has lived here since before man. Once, she was beautiful, a magnificent sight to behold. Now, she was a shriveled-up creature.

The weight of what Bill knew and what he allowed to happen had tarred his heart. If this rite was not honored as it had been done for thousands of years *She* would be offended.

One year many centuries ago, after the Catholics had built their churches and converted their flock, the locals had thought she was nothing more than an outdated legend. He suspected Fiona knew a great deal about magic. The woman was unnaturally old, she had been old when he first started working here and she was still alive. The Druids were a thing of the past, or so they thought.

Fiona had told him that one fateful year a sacrifice was not provided for the White Lady.

That same night she came above ground and fed on all their children as they slept. It was a morning never to be forgotten.

Now there was a whole city above to feed from.

Bill never got his true love, but he could help Garth find his if he did this one thing for him. Garth's the closest person Bill would ever have to a son, born to the woman he'd loved fiercely for thirty years.

CHAPTER TWENTY-TWO

Garth

Present Day: 20th March, 6:30 p.m.

Garth waited. Then waited some more. Cassie hadn't returned. Neither had Bill. He hung around the visitor center long after his shift ended. The caves had been shut for the day. The sun had sunk. A murder of crows had gathered, keeping watch from the trees above.

Takings for the day had been counted and bagged, the floors swept and cleaned three times by Garth trying to stick around, hoping to see Bill emerge with Cassie. The café across from the waiting area was dark and quiet. Ready for a new day.

Jenny, his manager, was there. She wouldn't even look at him. How could he have been so stupid?

People avoided him at school because he was a freak. He had the mark of loneliness upon him. He hadn't worn the right trainers at school. He had never been good at football or any sport. Had never been good with girls. He wasn't funny, others only laughed at him not with him. The kind of laughter that cut through him like a knife.

Other pupils could barely bring themselves to gaze at him surrounded by a crowd of loneliness at a time where kids only moved in packs. It was a terrible crime at school to have no friends. They feared Garth might be contagious, if anyone came within his space, they too would be a pariah casted out of society never to return to the flock.

He'd done nothing to deserve that treatment back then, but today he had.

He looked over at Jenny watching him sweeping the floor for the fourth time. Probably trying to restrain herself from shaking him violently for losing someone from his group.

No matter how much time passed, no one here was ever going to look back on this day and laugh about it. For Garth this would always be a mark of shame upon his character.

He had lost someone down in the caves. It was all his fault.

It was just the two of them now. She refused to talk. Her long thin cherry red nails rapping one by one on the counter like dancing spider legs. He imagined spiders coming towards their prey when their web has been sprung. He thought again of Cassie, trapped down there.

Jenny waited for Bill to resurface. He was taking his time. He was a trusted pair of hands. He took care of everything. Even still he should have returned hours ago, but he was a stubborn bastard. Much longer and he would be considered missing too.

Garth offered to wait for Bill to come back up in her place. He'd spent the last hour in the toilets crying, kept his eyes hidden so she couldn't see the inflamed red rims of his eyes. He needed to do something to help, not that he deserved the responsibility.

Even before this he felt like such a loser. He had no idea how much further he could sink in life.

"Go home," Jenny spoke quickly, as if it were offending her to address him. It was an order. Just his presence irritated her.

"I'm re—"

"Forget about what's happened here, we'll get it sorted. Go straight home." In a softer voice she looked across at him. It shocked him to have her look into his eyes. He'd spent so much of his life looking down avoiding others. She relaxed her stance almost smiled. "Don't tell anyone. We'll see what the morning brings."

Garth hated it that she hadn't shouted at him, called him an idiot, and really let rip. Why wouldn't she scream at him? He'd lost someone down in the caves. Someone who was so special and dear to him was in danger of losing their life. It was entirely his fault. In the history of the caves, this was the first time someone had been lost. That's how stupid he was. She should have yelled and grabbed at him. Hit him over and over like his dad would have done. That's what he was used to, but it wouldn't come forth.

He was stuck in purgatory.

The side door swung open. Garth had sworn he'd locked it. Couldn't he get anything right today?

The silence was swallowed up. A woman entered. Her black heels clipped loudly on the cold stone floor.

For a few moments Garth had considered her middle-aged based on her strength of stride, the way she held herself so high, but as she got closer, he saw she was old. Eighty at least.

He moved away from her, wanting to hide from her gaze in the dark café. Too late, she'd already seen him. Her mouth pressed hard together struggling to keep her thoughts unvoiced. She kept a careful watch on Garth, deciding eventually to say nothing, marching instead to Jenny standing to attention behind the counter.

"Fiona." Jenny did her best to look pleased to see the old lady, but her smile was unable to reach past her trembling mouth. "You didn't need to come. It's all being take care of. Bill's down there now, he'll be back any minute."

"What's being taken care of Jenny?"

Jenny stood back. "I overheard Bill saying someone had gone missing in the caves today."

"I didn't realize you knew." Fiona made her way behind the counter to where Jenny stood. "You allowed Bill to go down? I didn't want anyone to go down there looking. Not until I allow it. Do you have any idea what you've done?" Without turning to look at him Fiona pointed behind her to Garth. "Who is that?"

"Just someone who's been helping. He's leaving."

Before Garth took his cue, Fiona turned.

"You must be Garth." There was contempt in her voice but controlled like the waves set in her white hair. Unusually long for someone her age. It still shone. She would have been a formidable beauty. "You best be going, for now. But we may have need of you later, don't go far. You too, Jenny."

"I'll do anything to help," he said quickly before she changed her mind, bowing his head slightly as he walked out into the evening.

Garth ran out, closing the door with a neat click as he stepped outside. He cried again, couldn't have his boss of all people to see how much it hurt. Men weren't allowed to be weak, his dad taught him between the beatings that were supposed to toughen him up.

His battered car was the only one left in the car park. A chill night despite the pale advances of spring. He got in the drivers' seat.

He couldn't pin one solid reason why he liked Cassie so much. Why he couldn't stop thinking about her. There had been an instant connection. He'd felt something straightaway. She seemed different an outsider like him, but she could have been just like everyone else.

He was young, there would be others, he had the rest of his life to find someone, but yet …

Cassie.

She nagged on his thoughts. He had to find her. He couldn't leave without her. Not after what he had done. If he left, she would have no chance of survival.

In the darkness he saw her face, heard her laugh. She wouldn't leave him alone. The stain of her in his mind would never lift. Forever he'd be plagued by the what ifs.

What if she had said yes to a drink, said yes to a second date, said yes to being his girlfriend, yes to moving in, yes to settling down, yes to a family, yes to a life lived together?

What if that was what should have happened?

When he turned on the ignition and the lights, a dark mist coagulated around the car. He sniffed the air; it didn't smell like it was coming from the engine. It smelt like mushrooms.

It was cold and lonely out here, and for God's sake, Cassie was still down there. Right beneath his feet, alone in all that darkness that ran and ran for miles. What was she doing right now? Was she okay? He hoped she'd hadn't fallen in the darkness.

Had she panicked and made a wrong turn getting herself even more lost? Was she surrounded with ghosts playing tricks on her? There was no one with her to help her out. She was completely alone. The odds of survival stacked against her.

The human mind can't cope with complete darkness. Once plunged into total darkness there is nothing to guide you. You feel so puny and helpless against Death's dark eye when it spots you. Garth shivered. It had happened to him as part of his training being left to face it.

An uneasiness rooted in his belly. Looking up, he saw Fiona standing by the window sizing him up. How had she known his name? She didn't care that he knew she was staring at him like that, like she wanted to burn him. Why had Bill told her about Cassie going missing? Who was she?

There was something about her he didn't like, she was ancient yet youthful. She was completely in control of her face. Her command made her completely unreadable save for the fact she was cold. But those keen eyes suggested anger lay underneath. An anger that could easily erupt into violence. It was her eyes Garth liked least about her. Eyes that have seen more than a lifetime's worth of evil. In his car, behind a glass window, he felt a little safer against her glare. He stayed very still, crouching low in his seat until she decided to move away from the window and out of sight. He let out a long breath. What the fuck was that about? Who was that woman?

The darkness dripped down around him reminding him of what he'd done. He heard a voice like Cassie's, almost identical but not quite the same timbre. This voice was hardened with pain and eternal suffering.

"Save her."

"Hello? Who's there?" Garth looked around seeing no one.

Somebody was there, he just couldn't see them. He made up his mind, he had to do something to help find Cassie.

Chapter Twenty-Three

Garth

Present Day: March 20th, 6:45 p.m.

Garth couldn't leave Cassie down there. Not without a fight. He banged his fists against the steering wheel, bringing out his rage. Red clouds flooded his mind pushing his fear into retreat. He'd been holding the darkness back for years. He screamed a lone wolf's howl into the empty night.

The Garth of yesterday would have never dared to have spoken to Cassie. He would have been too scared to turn up for his first day at the caves.

But this was the new Garth.

He stepped out of his car, slamming the door behind him, not caring if it fell off. It was a piece of shit. At his age he should be able to afford something better. He shouldn't still be living at home either. Things needed to change.

Grabbing his rucksack from the boot he headed back in through a side door. He paused, held his breath to see if anyone had heard him enter.

Silently, he crept past. Keeping his movements slow he saw the back of Jenny's head sat in the office. She appeared to be fast asleep. Fiona was in the kitchen helping herself to the whisky hidden behind the microwave. He heard her put down her glass and refill it.

He edged open the doors.

Down he went.

The darkness got him every time, its grip on his body so much more noticeable when he was on his own. It wanted to hold him tight, bind him so that he couldn't run. This force would take his body and mind years to adapt to.

The mood of the caves was different when the darkness thought it was alone. No need to pretend it was only a lack of light.

Down here it was unleashed and free.

He took one last look at the outside world beyond the barred windows. The tunnel closed around him pushing him further in the depths of darkness. He would rather be at home sat in front of the TV catching up with his latest Netflix series but tonight he was going to be brave, for her. His Cassie.

He found no sign of Bill down here, the hero of the day. There was nothing Bill couldn't handle. He was a man forged of steel. Garth wanted to be like him one day: calm and collected, scared of nothing.

Garth was going to be the one to fix this, he wasn't a child anymore. He was a man. It was time he started living as one.

Very few people knew what true darkness was unless they had it in their heart. Especially here in London with 24/7 street lighting. Even deep in the last frontiers of ancient undisturbed lands such as Dartmoor, there were still stars burning a path of life through the void.

Garth knew true darkness. He'd known it from when he had first come here as a child. It had helped him on the day his father finally passed away. He was eternally grateful.

He'd had enough of the fear. Dad had destroyed his mother years ago, but he had been too young to realize what was going on, that it wasn't normal to live in that way, it wasn't right to treat someone so badly, especially when you've made an eternal vow of love and commitment. It took him a long time to understand that a real man protected the ones he loved.

He had been nothing but a little boy under his father's rule, too weak to make a stand and take on the burden of protecting his dear Mum. She grew weaker each day, that little fire inside her waning a little more. She was all he had in this life.

But he should have done something sooner.

Over the years, as his mother weakened, Garth grew and grew in strength, nourished by his mother's love and cooking. She always did what she could for him. Always weathered him from the storms of his father. There were times when his father paid him no attention, they were dangerous moments for her.

One day, Garth snapped.

Seeing his mum crying at the kitchen table, her hands shaking before her, unable to protect herself, too afraid to move or even breathe. Dad standing over her like an overgrown tree blocking out the sun. His guilty hands clenched and malformed with anger. There was blood sprayed on the floor. There was blood coming from the cut on Mum's cheek.

It had been the last straw. Garth went into the darkness, something inside him broke forever and snapped. He roared out all his hatred, telling his father exactly what he had been hiding all those years, how he hated him, but even more he hated himself for letting things come to this point.

There were words, heated exchanges and then his dad reached his fill and did what he always did when the dark anger took him. He lunged. This time for Garth.

But Garth went first, quicker, and stronger this time after all those years.

His dad fell back, turning red with anger, purple and then blue. Doctors said it had been a heart attack hastened by years of smoking and drinking.

Garth knew otherwise.

He'd put him in that grave. If he was honest, he felt a dark pride over it. The shame never came. That bothered him. If he had the chance, he'd do it again, and again. He only wished it had taken his father longer to die.

After the body was taken away, his mother slowly started to heal. Dad was never mentioned again. Family photos with Dad included were taken off the walls and replaced with new smiling ones. It was just the two of them. How it should have been.

The future was everything to live for and his mother was wasting no more time. She had taken up salsa, joined a book club, had her hair cut. Overnight she looked years younger. Even the house was brighter. It was safe. They were happy.

Today was the first day he'd felt that sense of shame returning. He had failed to protect his mother. He had failed to protect Cassie. His father had been right. Garth was a waste of space.

The sounds of men with their pickaxes hacking into the chalk woke him from his thoughts of self-loathing. He spun around trying to remember the way to the Druid's Altar, where he had last seen Cassie before she disappeared.

He'd lost all track of where he was, turning corner after corner. That's how the darkness got you down here.

Once it got inside your head it led you astray. Succumbing to it was a careless mistake but as much as he wanted to, he couldn't blame his father for this. He can't be always blaming his childhood for his present failings.

This was all on him.

He left the safe route. There were no more lights. The tunnels hung low over his head. Quickly, the walls gathered in. He hoped they wouldn't cave in on top of him, these tunnels were made of soft chalk, easily infiltrated by water and rain. There was rain forecast for later. But he had high hopes of finding her quickly. He must be in the Druid section, once his favorite area. Not anymore. He wished he could be anywhere else.

Under normal circumstances, he wouldn't be allowed here. But there was a missing girl. He doubted whether they would care. Why was Fiona so adamant no one should go down to look for Cassie?

Here was where legends were born. If he had a super-power, time travel would be his first choice. He'd use it to stop Cassie disappearing and come back here to when it was used as a dark church. Garth had been obsessed with history ever since he'd read about Merlin, Morgana, and Arthur, of their sorcery and strength, bravery and old magic. Magic had been a normal part of life. Now it was just social media.

He walked where the tunnels were crudely dug out, getting smaller and lower until crawling was necessary. Here marked the oldest part of the caves where it was least explored. The easiest place to get lost in, this could be where she was. He stopped to rest, trying to feel her presence through the airways, seeing if he had some sixth sense.

Aware that someone or something was watching him, he closed his eyes against the darkness of the cave.

Something passed by him, a ghost? It didn't linger. He became very cold, the same sensation he often felt when he'd done something bad.

It was too late to run. Even if he knew the way back from here, he couldn't leave Cassie in the darkness, the same darkness he'd kept his mum in for all those years.

He had come here because he had led Cassie into this, he must be the one to bring her out.

CHAPTER TWENTY- FOUR

Sienna

Present Day: March 20th, 6:20 p.m.

"Aren't you even going to ask for my name?"

Fiona barely looked at her. Still confined to the table, Sienna's forehead beaded with pain induced sweat. She was keeping the horror all inside. No one was going to get the satisfaction of seeing Sienna suffer.

Who knew that being held captive with rope could elicit so much suffering on her body? Today she had learnt so much of human physiology and pain. She had lost the feeling in her arms long ago, even the pain had gone, or maybe she was too used to it. Had her nerve endings been permanently damaged? Would she ever walk again?

Without turning her back, Fiona continued to sweep the room, picking up with great distaste a long brown hair belonging to Sienna. She was making sure that soon there would be no trace of her being here.

"I already know your name, Melanie."

Sienna lifted her head to look at Fiona. How did this woman know her real name was Melanie? She couldn't do anything other than scream, which she did even though it burned her throat with acidic bile.

The dryness burned and cracked what little voice she had left. She let the anger take over, it was better than being scared.

Fiona left without looking back.

Sienna lay back exhausted.

Melanie.

Sienna's life started out much like any other girl. She had dreams and a big heart. Sienna wasn't special, even though she thought she was, just one of many that Fiona could have chosen.

Her dreams grew and grew until Sienna was forced to obey them. Her curse was her beauty. She felt because of it she deserved to be adored and loved by millions. It became her calling. She wanted to sing, act, dance, anything to have all the attention of adoration on her. She wanted people to look at her and cry with envy. Wanted to steal the shine of everyone looking at her.

Except no one noticed her after her baby sister was born Maura. A prettier version, a girl who laughed her way into everybody's heart. A child even a heartless mother could love. Melanie grew tired of competing against a better girl. Grew tired of being overlooked. So, she changed, she became Sienna.

One day, their father took them to the beach by their little seaside town. He relaxed under the sun with a paper whilst their mother caught up with chores at home.

Sienna saw her chance when dear little Maura got into difficulty during their swim, her little head barely able to bob above the water's surface. *Melanie* hadn't needed to do anything. The tide did it all.

When Maura finally returned to the shore, face down in the calm crystal waters, the deed was done.

Her father was broken that day, he drank himself to death after his wife kicked him out. Melanie's mother now loved her remaining daughter more than ever. They became so close, but mothers eventually live out their usefulness.

Aged eighteen, Melanie officially became Sienna, a beautiful headstrong woman bound for London. She cut all ties. Changing her name meant no one could come looking for her. She found a rich man, then another and another. The married ones were the best choices for advancement.

The career of being famous never took off but she had something better: money, power, and a cloak of invisibility. Or so she thought. She lived a life of such fun. Stealing was easy. She had ruined so many lives, marriages, and childhoods. Until she got caught by Fiona.

How did Fiona know her real name? She hadn't been called Melanie for over ten years. No one living could have known that. What else did she know? She must think, but thinking was so hard to do when your body was slowly shutting down. Fiona hadn't even given her a drop of water to drink. If she didn't escape this room, she would certainly die at her hands.

It was useful to try and figure what this old woman wanted. It seemed too personal that she was snatched off the streets for human trafficking. Fiona knew her. She wanted revenge. Maybe Fiona was a distant relative? Did she know about Maura?

Sienna shook her head, tried to kick her legs. Even wriggle her big toe. Nothing. Why was she being held like this?

It wasn't her fault. She was only a child back then. There was nothing wrong with ruthless ambition.

Maura, her sister would have been twenty-two if she hadn't drowned.

Her sister. Despite it all Maura had really looked up to Melanie and she had wanted to please her the most. It was hard for her to think of anything else when being held in a small dark room underground. Being held so close to death forced a person to re-examine all their mistakes, big and small. She began to cry. This was it. She was going to die alone.

Just like her sister.

She screamed again. She'd been running from it her whole life. Now it was catching up.

A sniggering in the corner jolted Sienna to her senses. There was someone there. It wasn't Fiona. She would never so much as smile unless it was to watch someone die.

Sienna raised her head from the table just enough to see Fiona's son standing in the corner of the room. He must have hidden behind the door where Fiona couldn't have seen him. She'd sent him away hours ago.

"No one knew I was here." He straightened himself out with pride. Standing as tall as his hunched back would allow. The son was as weak as his mother was strong. He was a simpleton. Soft like butter.

"Very clever to fool your mother like that." She lay her head back down on the wooden table resting the screaming vertebrae in her neck. "Does she ever let you upstairs?"

He leaned over her with his thumbs up. His meaty breath escaping from his brown jagged teeth was nauseating. It took him a while to understand what she was saying. After the third repeat he giggled like a clown.

"I like it down here. One day, Mother said she'll let me see *her* again. I'm much older than you."

He was mental but she had to hold on. She could use him to help her escape. "Her? Lovely. Tell me more."

He giggled again; he was too old to giggle. "You'll meet her soon." He ran his rough hand along her bare leg pockmarked with cold. "She'll like you a lot."

Sienna bit back against the need to scream at him for touching her. She must keep him on side. She wore a smile to mask her fear. "Can you tell me where I am?"

"You're in our house."

"Where?"

"In the cellar, my favorite place." He gave Sienna a good view of his yellow and brown misshapen teeth. "There's secrets in there."

She forced a smile. "Secrets? Can you tell me one?"

"I'm not allowed too close."

"Why am I here? Why I'm so special?"

"Mother chose you. Because of what you did. Mother always finds out. She keeps eyes on everyone. Mother has been watching you for a long time. What we do here is very important. Mother must make sure only those who deserve to be down there go. Mother is happy that no one is going to miss you."

"Look, I'll change. Can you get your mother back in here? I'll be good. I'll do anything. Somehow being here has made me closer to God. I feel a connection with Him. Let me live and I'll serve him with love and devotion." She had been counting on him as a religious maniac.

Instead, he laughed. "It's not a God down there."

Sienna had a new idea.

The son wrinkled his nose, waving his hands around to clear and clean the air around him. "Poo-ey."

"I need to go to the toilet," Sienna said noting his embarrassment. "It's coming, and I can't hold it in much longer."

"No, you mustn't." He looked to the door anxiously. "There's no time to clean you again."

Sienna kept her face serene as he looked around. Another came forth. He didn't want to untie her, but he knew it would make a terrible mess if she shat on the table.

"You could go toilet in the corner. Mother has locked the door. We can't get out," he eventually said.

She made no move; she might not be able to. If he needed to help her off the table, then she had little chance of escape. There must be something in here that could be used against him as a weapon.

He began to free her limbs, legs first. They moved like heavy joints of ham when she tried to lift them off the table. Sensation rushed in an angry torrent of tiny ants biting her veins as they moved through. She slowly wriggled her toes; all her bones were crunching. She needed a few more seconds for them to work again.

Her arms, held for hours in an unnatural position, were going to be the problem. But at least she could run if she made it out of this hellish chamber.

A chance appeared. An ugly one but she took it. She had no choice when he made the mistake of getting too close to her. Moving in so he could untie the rope around her arms. They were so close she could see a big vein beating in his neck. It excited him to feel her so close to him.

It was too tempting.

She flew up and clenched down into his neck with her teeth until her jaws threatened to crack apart her back teeth.

Those useless canines missed his neck entirely but there was something fleshy and hard in her mouth that wasn't her own. Warm salty blood swirled around in her mouth. She spat it out along with a small piece of something chewy like Haribo.

Making a small whimpering sound he ran back into the corner behind the door. Before he had a chance to turn angry, she took a wooden bowl from Fiona's work bench and hit him on the back of his head.

It felt so good.

The movement brought back the power to her arms. Soon each strike was hitting jelly after the bone cracked open. His movements became jerky. A robot losing control. Slower and slower. She stopped when she could no longer make out his head.

He screamed no more.

A white cotton dress had been laid out. Quickly she took it and put it on. She rattled the handle of the door which Fiona used to come in and out. This door must lead back up to the house.

He was right. It was locked, but in the corner of the room there was another door. An old door, not tall enough for a modern human to pass through, but anything was better than being in this room. Fiona wasn't going to be jovial when she came back to find her son reduced to a meat trifle.

Sienna cried out when the other door opened, the passageway sealed with thick white spiderwebs. There was no time to be scared or repulsed. It led into darkness where the air was damp. It smelt of rotting mushrooms. Sienna felt confused it appeared to lead down rather than out.

Her goal was to escape this hell hole and find help, not get further lost within this hellhole. The walls were too narrow. She could get stuck and not be able to turn herself around. This didn't seem right, but what else could she do? Turn back? Wait for Fiona to return?

Going down was the only option of escape that she had.

She took the large burning candle sheltering the flame with her hands. The feeble light tried to make its way into the darkness.

Knowing she didn't have long, she stepped in. The passageway was steep, it wound downwards. Not the direction she wanted to take, but it put distance between her and that mad witch up above.

Affording herself one last look at the room she had been held in, proving to herself again she was a born survivor, Sienna made a salute and smiled grimly at the mess in the corner.

"I hope you saw that, Fiona."

CHAPTER TWENTY-FIVE

Cassie

Present Day: March 20th, 6:45 p.m.

Cassie's mind felt separated from her body. The rush of freedom exhilarated her. She wasn't suffering with grief down here. With Death so close it didn't feel like an ending anymore. Down here death was just another phase of being. Her sister was simply gone, and now coming to the caves, it was possible for Cassie to find her.

Her feet shuffled carefully on the floor as if the rock beneath might suddenly give way to nothingness in this topsy turvy world. Her hands reached out but couldn't find solid rock. Her fingers unable to find the sides of the soft damp tunnels leading deeper.

She waded into the deep dark until there was nothing to bring her back, no familiar smell, sight, sound, anything that could anchor her back to her own world high above her head. This was all she knew now.

Here was where deep magic circulated. The feeling of forgotten knowledge being revealed only to her was luxurious; she breathed it in, as much as her lungs could hold until they weighed heavy with ancient wisdom. The darkness shimmered around her and hummed. *Soon,* she thought, *if she stayed here long enough, she'd be able to understand what the darkness wanted to say to her.* Maybe she could learn to control it? It was tempting.

Cassie couldn't remember how the idea about coming here alone came to her. Maybe a voice in her head had told her to? She had only planned as far as getting down here, she hadn't yet thought about how she was going to find her way back up after she had spoken with her dead sister Hayley. She wasn't sure if she ever wanted to leave. Now she was in the Otherworld. Truly. She was sure of it. An ancient realm still revered by long forgotten ancestors. The realm of the dead watched over by ancient deities. Passage only granted at certain times of the year through burial mounds, hollow hills, or endless caves. In her bones she felt its power keenest.

Once this had been a site of worship. When she stood quiet, she could hear the last echoes of their songs keeping alive old strange memories of ancients gathering in candle lit processions, burning white winter flowers laid to rest on cold stones. They came here often to mark the sabbaths and the ever-turning wheel of life. *They* would remember always.

It passed to her.

Although dark and quiet and buried under modern day Britain, the caves remained an active realm. Death never dies, it endures.

In every nook, every congealed spot of darkness, every hollow there was a sense of furtiveness, of things rushing here and there underfoot, a plane of existence undetected by Cassie.

Until now.

This was a different world almost in alignment with hers, she concluded, as alien to human life as the cold bright moon way up high. Down here was the source of the darkness that waited for us underneath. The current that took people under.

She needed to remain calm.

There was no need to pretend she had been coping after Hayley's suicide. No one was here to see or hear her cry. She'd offered up herself to the darkness. It had answered. From every direction it rushed towards her coming to feed, picking her clean and ready to face the world again.

She'd been given a gift.

When she re-emerged back into the light of life from this dark womb she would be unburdened from guilt for her dead sister.

She would be Cassie again, not this wraith like creature hiding from the world. She could begin again, be brand new, a new Cassie stronger than before. A kinder version who never hurt anyone. A new life free of guilt and shame.

She was ready to confront her guilt and bury it once and for all down here, where it belonged amongst the dead and the dust in the empty caverns.

Cassie should have done more to help. She should have been kinder, should have forced Hayley to open up to her and listen. She should have made Hayley get help, if she had done so, Hayley could still be alive.

Being so close to death, she'd never felt so alive. A power coursed through her, reaching every cell. With death came renewal.

Her plan was working.

In the darkness she saw clearly. She still had her whole life ahead of her. As long as warm blood swam in her veins and her heartbeat, she could do anything.

If she could dream it, she could make it happen. Magic was the joy of being alive, of being able to seek and invoke change.

All that was left to do down here was to find Hayley and leave. When she was back up on land, she would be a better person.

Hayley could be in any one of these tunnels closing in on her. Cassie swiveled her torch upwards. She glanced away when she saw how low the ceilings were. The tunnels became constrictive, soon they would be too narrow to walk through. Not even her feet made echoes on the dimpled floor. Why were there no echoes here?

She could be floating. She could be dead. She'd believe it if it wasn't for the drumming in her chest, the calming rhythm of breathing in and out without pain reminding her to hold on until she re-emerged.

Cassie wasn't scared. She wasn't alone anymore. The spirits were coming. Hayley would soon be here. Yet she daren't call out her name. She heard them all in the walls. There was something creeping behind her, out of sight. It had come to watch her.

She knew who it was.

Chapter Twenty-Six

Cassie

Present Day: March 20th, 6:50 p.m.

At last, her sister had returned to her. A clemency after death. Cassie understood. She'd been a terrible sister, and a terrible person after all these years. The things you didn't do was what hurt others the most.

All those kind words she never said which could have saved Hayley. All those hugs she didn't give out when her twin needed a little warmth. She could have given her more time. Shown a little love. But it was too late. Cassie fought back tears. Why couldn't she have realized this sooner when Hayley was still alive?

Beneath the streets of London, she had the chance to say sorry. Sorry for being the favorite twin who stole all the glory. She never found it hard to be a good daughter, a clever student, a high achiever. It was only being a good sister that had been impossible.

Life was never the same after Hayley had wandered off in the caves. After she began to change after her visit to the caves. She spent hours in her room by herself. The door was always locked. Hayley was always overlooked by their parents, and it was all her fault. Cassie was always too eager to be loved and adored.

Now she saw why Hayley was always so upset with her, why she turned to Cassie to put things right. It's so hard to be an individual when you are a clone of a person who will always be superior to you.

A voice came out of the ether and landed in her ear. "Now you see."

Cassie stopped. It had worked. She wiped a tear from her eye and spun round. Hayley was nearer than she had ever been. So close, she could step through the veil separating their worlds. She smiled to know she was right; they still had that connection. Hayley could still get inside her head. At least she could know now just how sorry Cassie was.

At last, Hayley.

"I wanted to say I'm sorry Hayley, for everything." Cassie treasuring the moment put out her hands, but no embrace came. She had never felt so cold.

"Hayley?" Where was she?

A caress soft and tender, like silk, brushed against her cheek. Her body trembled from the feet upwards rising fast like a tide to her mind.

Cassie had to keep it together despite being overcome with feelings of revulsion. Her teeth chattered. What would Hayley look like now? Cassie shone the torch and saw only darkness.

What was happening to her? Cassie couldn't move. She was nothing, a tiny mortal trapped in an immortal realm. A soft spring breeze trapped within a winter storm.

A cold hand wrapped around her neck, affording her generous breath but nothing else.

"Bring me back. I want to come home." Hayley's voice had accumulated twenty-three years of hurt.

"How?"

"I want to go home. Why didn't you come sooner?"

Hayley would spend eternity here. She could never go back home. That life was gone and all she had was this, the embrace of darkness.

"I'm so cold and hungry Cass. Did you bring food and blankets?"

"Hayley." Cassie took a deep breath, trying to stay afloat, her body swaying caught the dark undertow. "You need to hear this."

"What is it you want to tell me?"

"I'm sorry."

"Cassie, help me. Bring me home. Give me your hand."

The black mist condensed.

"Hayley, I can't. You're dead." She bit her bottom lip. Pain brought comfort.

"Help me, Cass."

The sensation around her neck loosened, the grip subsided. "I came here to say sorry for all the things I did and didn't do."

"Bring me back."

"But I also came to say goodbye." Cassie managed to finish her sentence before her voice broke. She carried on in a whisper. "I can't bring you back."

"What? Why won't you help me?"

There was constriction around her neck again. This was the dark side of her sister, the side of her that could never be happy, never be calmed and now it was all that remained.

"I am tired. I haven't slept in months. I hate it here and you come here to tell me I can't leave?"

"I'm sorry, Hayley." That pitiful word was all she could manage as she hung in her dead sister's chokehold.

"You must take me back." She lowered her voice so only Cassie could hear. "Away from *her*."

"Her?"

"I'm not alone. We are not alone Cassie. This is her home."

"What are you talking about?"

"Help me, Cassie."

"You know I can't. Why don't you ever listen to me?"

There was silence. There was nothing and then Cassie was thrown against a wall spiked with sharp juts of flint. She yelped in pain. Her vision swam, she must have hit her head. Her skin split with hot pain.

Cassie didn't need to see her arm to know it was deep. Warm blood trickled down her face. It was going to need medical attention when she got out of the caves. She started to step backwards slowly so as not to cause alarm. Hayley held her back against the wall, her force weaker, less malevolent.

"Who else is here Hayley?"

"You've cut yourself," Hayley chided. "What have you done Cassie? She's going to find you."

An orchestra of whispers of the other trapped spirits built up around her in the darkness. Each of them had their face carved on the walls, completely claimed by the White Lady. They could never leave, but Cassie still had a choice.

"The White Lady has woken, she's on her way," the voice of a young boy warned.

"Who's the White Lady?" Cassie asked. She was growing weak. She wanted to stand but everything was spinning too fast. If she moved too quickly, she would throw up.

"Hurry, she's coming. She's already caught your scent."

Cassie couldn't reply, her vision changed to pixelated fractals of light swirling around her. She fell into the darkness landing on the floor, unconscious. Her torch which had been held tight in her hand rolled away.

Chapter Twenty-Seven

Garth

Present Day: March 20th, 7:45 p.m.

He had heard nothing in the caves for the past hour except for the constant screaming in his head. The shame of his mistakes weighing him down keeping him under. Cassie. He'd led her down there. Would he ever find her? Would he ever reach the surface?

He shook his head and told himself off. *What the fuck am I doing?* It was madness to come here looking for a girl he barely knew.

But wasn't that how love worked? Falling in love was a life changing condition that made little sense. Only that he knew he would rather give his life to save hers than live without her. He couldn't believe how easily he had fallen head over heels for her, but it had happened. That's why he couldn't stop thinking about her.

Where was Cassie?

Bone achingly cold, his stomach rumbled in anger, curling up in angry contortions threatening to eat itself. This cave was not meant for his kind.

At breakfast he'd been too nervous for his Sugar Puffs. By lunchtime he was too sick with shame to eat, by dinner time there were more pressing matters to attend to.

Cassie.

He grew angrier with each passing minute, in the absence of light each one stretched into an hour. How long would he have to spend down here?

He checked his watch. He had been there for just over two hours, but it felt like even his watch was playing tricks on him. It felt possible he'd been here all night. Ever since he went through those doors his mind had been in some strange sleeping state. This couldn't be real; this wasn't happening to him.

Any minute now he'd wake up and see this was all a dream.

Death was forever chasing at one's heals. Down here it was at its very strongest.

There were no earthly rules within these passages governed by dark forces. These caves made him feel alien with his weak soft skin, the need for air, not only needing to see light but to feel it on his skin.

To be human is to feel the weakness of your body as it slowly wanes year on year to broken bones and dust.

It was like he was at the very bottom of the ocean, everything pressing down on him. The darkness alone would kill him if he couldn't find a way out.

He'd ran down consumed only with the pursuit of the one hope in his future; Cassie, the girl who could change everything about him. No one knew he was here. His mum would have made him dinner. Now she would be sat alone waiting at an empty table. Wondering why he wasn't home.

Who was going to come and find him?

He wasn't ready to admit it yet, but he was lost without hope.

She's still not here, with him.

This wasn't the sort of place where you could call out for help. The darkness swallowed all sounds. It behaved differently down here. Moving like a hungry fog, he felt black energy brush against his face tugging at his clothes, creeping up his legs.

The darkness wanted to keep him here. If he were to collapse … but he kept moving through the ancient fog.

Dad was waiting for him down here.

In the darkness, he saw his father's snarling twisted face in each shadow that pounced upon him. Intangible forces that made his forehead hot and stomach queasy whenever they made contact.

126

What were those things?

The guilt was hammering on his door, wood splintering in shards of shame. He was completely alone. It was time to face the truth that he could have stopped Dad much earlier if he had been braver. Even as a boy he could have protected his mum. But he hadn't. Now it was too late.

Dad may be dead, but he'd never leave Garth alone. He kept seeing him in the cave, forcing him to face his past with each day. What had taken him so long to act? He hadn't protected his mother from his father's anger.

All those things Dad said about him were right. He was weak. He was an embarrassment. All those times he watched Dad beat Mum from under the kitchen table or squatting behind the sofa. He could have been a better son and looked after her. But he wasn't.

There was no sign of Bill. Garth had been hoping that he would have bumped into him as soon as he got here. They would have found her together. There was not even the distant echo of Bill's heavy self-assured footsteps trundling along. What was Bill doing down here? He must have stepped away from the safe route.

Garth had been told time and time again. Never venture off the route. Only step where there were lights overhead.

He had asked whether it was because there were risks the cave could collapse. Was it prone to flooding after a heavy downpour of English rain?

But all that was given to him was the admission that there were many things they still did not know about the caves. Even today, no one had any idea how far the tunnels went on for—no-one but the people who had dug these out thousands of years ago. He wondered what had happened to them.

Not even the old boys ventured away from the route. Going off track was never joked about; it was an abomination as stupid as coming down here without a torch. Leaving the designated paths illuminated with overhead lights would place him in danger.

Cassie was still nowhere to be found.

She didn't realize the situation she was in. He felt shameful for taking away her lantern. He shouldn't be here in the safe zone when she was out there. All alone.

He had no right to feel safe when he put his mother through hell. Now he was doing it to Cassie. It was a pattern he had to break, even if it meant giving up his life.

Today was the day he was going to change.

He stepped into the swilling darkness, down a narrow tunnel winding downwards like a helter-skelter. Here it was much colder his breath misted around him. In Garth's mind there was no dispute of ghosts existing here, if they had a nest, he was fast approaching it.

The air on his tongue tasted thick. It was getting harder to breathe. The ground became uneven constantly throwing him off balance. He was sliding deeper down. Would this never end? Something in his way made him fall.

"Somebody help me," he cried.

But he was the help.

Voices of the dead conversed around him, he caught snippets of their conversations, of sermons given under the white cross erected in the makeshift cave chapel, praying for peace and an end to the death and destruction, of people rushing to their bunks before the bombs hit, children sneaking out in the darkness playing hide-and-seek while the world held its breath. Everything down here grated on him. He wanted to be outside in the fresh air.

"You'll never find her." His father's gravelly snarling voice found him. "It's all your fault, you stupid boy."

"Leave me alone you monster." As he scrambled through the darkness, he felt a hand grab his ankle. His father was trying to drag him back. Even in death he still hated his son, felt no guilt for the father he had been,

"I hate you," Garth roared as he kicked his way away from him vowing to never think of him again.

He crawled out of the tunnel. Here he was. At the Druid's Altar. How had he only made it this far?

This wasn't going to plan. But at least his father had stopped chasing him. The dead had evaporated. Silence lay all around, no ghosts would come near this place.

The light bounced in and around the dugout cove. He stared hard hoping for a clue, were those claw marks around the base? What caused those dark spots seeping in the rock, blood or rust? His father was right after all. He was in too deep to call for help. Someone had been hurt here. He was no closer to finding Cassie or Bill. Now he was afraid for himself too.

He really shouldn't be here; he was trespassing over ancient territory.

Leave this spot to the Old Ones.

What had held him so enthralled all these years?

This had always been his favorite spot, but he stood here knowing he'd never again sleep with the lights off. His insides trembled with weakness.

Even if he got out of here, what would his life be like now? The pain of a life lived wrong throbbed in his chest. He should have done things differently. He saw it with painful clarity. He'd wasted so many years for nothing.

There wasn't a reset button. There never is.

The altar had been decorated.

It was still being used.

CHAPTER TWENTY-EIGHT

Garth

Present Day: March 20th, 8:00 p.m.

On the Druid's Altar, dark red apples had been arranged on a chalk drawn pentagram, a strange black mist circulated above, millions of eyes watching, waiting. One by one they began to swivel to where he stood.

Next to it were dead blackbirds with their wings splayed open like fans, their legs and feet curled up in defeat. Silver jewelry shined molten around burning incense.

Pale bulbous mushrooms had been left in a wicker basket, dark red berries with black insides rotted in an earthenware pot. Another bowl held a wriggling mess of worms, a feast for the dead.

Garth couldn't bear to look upon those worms. Blind little things lost inside a dark mezzanine. They could never hope to find their way out, to try would be futile. Poor things. The thought of spending an eternity in these caves …

He couldn't make sense of the fact that someone else had been down here. It was possible. There were many hidden points of entry, most of the abandoned mineshafts reached out into people's gardens. Was this a kid's prank? Bill? Or was it the work of someone else? Garth looked behind him. Who else was down here?

Cassie might be involved with some weird shit. It might be wiser to run from her, in case this was all a trap. It all made sense, she had charmed the pants off him then disappeared abruptly.

He'd never understood women. Men had brawn and might, but women had something else entirely. Their strength ran deeper, endured beyond what mortals could carry on their shoulders. When their eyes met across the room earlier had she chosen him for a macabre purpose?

Behind him was the long corridor, the ancient route of the Druid procession. The source of the darkness. He'd been thinking about this spot all day.

This is where he last saw Cassie. Where he asked her out for a drink. He remembered that part, that feeling of giddy excitement giving way to hope.

She must have gone down there. The darkest part of the caves. What on earth had possessed her?

He must follow.

Since boyhood, Garth had dreamt of the day when he could go off exploring like Indiana Jones, his childhood hero, into the depths of the unknown. Twenty years later his dream exposed to reality had turned sour.

Now deep into this subterranean abyss, all his desire for adventure and adrenaline was gone. He just wanted to relax on the sofa nursing a hot chocolate with Mum, watching cheesy horror films.

The torch rattled in his hand.

He didn't need eyes in the back of his head to know he was being watched. The shadows were playing tricks on him. He'd never felt so exposed in his entire life.

There was something here.

Here right where he stood were no sound of ghosts. They'd all fled when he got to the altar. It was just him that remained.

His body urged him to turn back. Do what he'd always done in life, run away and hide. It'd kept him alive so far.

Not today.

Cassie urged him forward; he was going to find her.

Up ahead there was ragged breathing on the path that went deep down. It was coming towards him. He stopped and listened.

He reminded himself there was nothing down here except him, Bill and Cassie. It had to be one of them.

"Cassie?" his voice came out scared. No, he had to be the hero today. She could be injured. Maybe she'd fallen and banged her head. She could be suffering in terrible pain.

Maybe she was dead.

He cleared his throat, hiding the fear in his voice. "Cassie?" Louder, clearer. Shit. He sounded like an angry dad, not a look he was going for.

A dark mass took shape, coagulating in the corner of his eye. Was he seeing things? He flashed his torch to it, whatever it was leapt from sight before he could see.

"What the fuck?"

That was an animal. Sometimes birds got trapped down here but no bird he'd heard of could be that big.

The only living thing down here were mushrooms. The hairs on his arms rose, a coldness beckoned like a dead lover refusing to release their grip

"Hello?"

He wasn't alone. The approaching darkness smothered him completely like a mother's love. There was something beside him stealthily closing in.

All his preternatural senses urged him to run. His torch searched the tunnel floor. Nothing. Above him a scraping sound, it was coming from the ceiling. There weren't bats living here.

Then slowly, he raised the torch. His eyes sweeping upwards opening wide. His mouth went dry, his tongue poised to scream.

His eyes didn't want to believe it.

Maybe it once been human. It had two arms and legs but that's where the similarities ended. Long hair hung down.

On the ceiling directly above was a creature swaddled in its own limbs staring at him with hatred. Hatred was what kept the creature alive, helped it to function. A hate that wanted to destroy the light, wanted to destroy every last scrap of humanity and beyond until there was nothing but dark oblivion.

Briefly in its face he saw his father contorted with everlasting rage and anger. Or maybe what he was seeing was his own deepest fears being projected onto the creature because when he blinked the creature changed.

Those black unblinking eyes stared down at him full of hate and hunger. Its skin was sickly white, mottled blue. The creature was alive but looked like it had been laying in a morgue for months. Was this why Bill wouldn't let Garth look for Cassie. Was Bill trying to protect him all along?

Maybe it had been human but now it was too far gone. Its spindly limbs elongated and stretched. So thin they looked could snap anytime but Garth sensed its unrivalled strength. Scuttling with the agility of a spider, running upside along walls. Its long brown hard nails easily able to hold on to the cave walls.

Garth's mouth hung open; his stomach flipped. The creature switched between images of itself, a pale woman and then of his dad's face turning molten red and pulsating with anger. Just before the onslaught of blows came raining down. Each one harder than the previous until his father would be spent and he'd either leave for the pub or go out through the kitchen door where his shed stood at the bottom of the garden.

The creature grinned down at him. When it laughed a cold shiver lit up all the nerves in his body. How could it have known that? Was that how the creature fed? Feeding off the fear of the people who came here.

It knew Garth. He ran his hand through his hair, somehow it all made sense. This creature knew everything. All those painful memories and fears he had released into the darkness when he was younger. All that pain had to go somewhere.

How long had she been watching him? Minutes or years?

He flashed the torch directly at it. It hissed and retreated. Its emaciated arms and legs shuttling backwards like a spider, retreating into a shadow. She remained close to him, just beyond the reaches of his torch. Not far enough to make him feel safe. At least he had a weapon against it.

It wasn't going to give up. The thing wanted something from him. Was it hungry? Unfortunately, he hadn't brought any food to assuage it.

It tried to approach him side on but was pushed back when he moved his beam of light. Its black dripping lips snarled in rage.

It was hard to see the face properly upside down, but he was sure it was female. An elderly woman whose fragility had been replaced with strength.

"Today is the day I fight back."

He couldn't let that thing anywhere near Cassie.

She was still out there. She needed him.

Keeping his torch positioned on the creature he acted fast. He took out a handheld flare from his rucksack. He'd bought it as a joke from a shop thinking he'd never use it, that it was something fun to have in the boot of his car.

It exploded into red bonfire light that burned his brain. The place looked like the bowels of Hell. Every sharp jut of rock illuminated in cherry red.

Garth was thrown backwards by it. Beyond the red light he couldn't see. The creature's scream echoed as it fled.

It was gone, hopefully he'd injured it.

Warm urine dripped down his leg pooling around his feet. The shaking throughout his weak body was unbearable. The only force keeping him going was his adrenaline.

"Cassie!" he roared into the darkness. There was nothing else here, just him and that thing. He crouched by the flare. Too tired to walk. Only weak enough to wait for the love of his miserable little life to return.

CHAPTER TWENTY-NINE

Cassie

Present Day: March 20th, 8:00 p.m.

When Cassie woke up, she was sure someone had just shouted her name. It sounded like a young man, she prayed it was Garth. Lost and alone in the darkness feeding off her fear it felt wonderful to have someone thinking of her. That somebody cared, enough to follow her into the darkness.

But the sound of approaching footsteps never came.

Unnatural coldness seeped through her skin. Her surroundings were still a mystery to her. Not that it mattered. There was no way out. This is where she belonged.

Every part of her ached as if she'd been thrown down a well. She should have stayed in bed this morning. A whole day lying in bed feeling miserable suddenly seemed the idea of heaven.

Instead of being here counting down her final moments on earth, she could have been warm and wrapped up, eating takeaway pizza whilst watching Netflix. Cassie could have been safe.

She had been lying on her side. Her hips ached as she shuffled to find comfort, but none was to be found. Across from her there was a light trying to shine through a dark settled mist.

Her torch.

Then she remembered. She was in the caves. Lost. She'd found Hayley beyond the grave. Death proved no barrier to her built up rage and resentment.

Cassie needed to get back up into the sunlight but how?

Her sister warned from the darkness. "Run, she's coming for you. Stay away from the darkness."

"Hello?" Cassie shifted into a sitting position; her head throbbed worse than any headache she'd ever endured. It was too early to assess all the damage.

Cassie crawled along the soft damp floor hoping not to set off more pain in her body, her right arm reaching for the torch lying close by.

She shuffled then waited in silence to check the only noises here were the ones coming from her suffering. Her fingers wrapped around her only chance of survival. She pulled the torch to her chest as she rested on her back taking deep breaths for the exertion. She cradled it as if it were the holy grail. Having light down here made her feel strong again.

"Hayley is that you? Are you there?"

Cassie had no idea how long she had been out for. Time moved differently here without the sun to mark its passage. She could have been here her entire life. She could barely remember the world up there. She fought back tears. She needed to conserve her water. What was she thinking coming down here by herself?

But she wasn't alone.

Someone was beside her as she laid spent on the cave floor. It wasn't Hayley. Had someone come back to save her?

Despite their differences, they'd always had a special twin bond, a weird connection that bound them, even to this day, but this presence wasn't that. It was alien.

A voice in the darkness swirled around Cassie. She shone her torch in the direction of the presence where underground mist assembled. All around her was cold stone, narrow tunnels teasing her sense of direction and of course, the darkness.

"Come to me, sister." A raspy voice came out of the gloom.

"Hayley?"

Could it be Hayley? Had death changed her? What was she going to do now? What did she want? Was she ever going to let Cassie go?

It had been stupid to think she could see Hayley one last time. That she could ever overcome her grief for her dead twin sister. The pain of losing her was going to hurt every day for the rest of her life.

There was no way to help Hayley. Death should be a respite from pain and illness, but Hayley still suffers, she will always suffer. Hayley will never leave this place.

Cassie stayed still waiting where the voice came from. She wasn't ready to say goodbye. Just one last hug. Anything for that last glimpse of the sister she had lost.

Cassie felt robbed of her happy ending but what did she really expect? That Hayley would have come running into her arms and they'd go back together into the sunlight hand in hand. Life doesn't have a happy ending. It endures until the darkness catches you.

"You came back, sweet sister."

"Hayley, where are you? Please let me see you. Can we hug it out?"

"Cassie, I'm scared. You must leave."

There were two distinct voices trying to communicate with Cassie. Each with different commands. One coming from the darkness of the caves, another one coming from inside Cassie's mind.

Which one was Hayley's?

Who did the other voice belong to?

"Hayley, you're safe now. There's nothing to fear anymore. Everything is finished, it's all over. You've passed, nothing can get near you again."

"Cassie, you have no idea. Just get out."

"Sweet sister, turn off the light, come closer, we can be together."

Cassie swung the torch to and fro. Had the tunnels moved? Something was different. She was sure she'd been sitting opposite two tunnels, now there were three.

Why wouldn't Hayley come back to her? Just one last time? That's all she wanted.

The beam made paltry headway into the darkness. Black stopped the beam of light like a solid brick wall. The texture of the darkness was changing. Her eyes saw nothing of her sister, not even an opaque outline or a human-shaped cloud of mist. Seeing nothing yet knowing something is there was worse.

This was a punishment. Hayley could be so cruel.

Bits of gravel dislodged around her, scrabblings of loose chalk and flint came from all directions. Loose scree hitting her head and shoulders. It was the first noise, other than the voices, she heard that hadn't been made by her. What was above her?

"Hayley? Is that you?" Cassie stood still. Surely, she was safely hidden in the darkness.

Was Hayley watching her from within the darkness? Had she come to unleash the full force of Cassie's suffering. There seemed to be no desire from her for a rekindling of sweet sisterly love.

Something spindly and sharp like metal scraped against the soft rock, cutting in and grinding. Cassie could only hear it. She flashed her torch in the offending direction seeing only a slight blur of something unearthly creep away. Too quick for her eyes to capture its image. What followed was a complete silence as if all life had ceased to exist.

"I love you Cassie, I'm sorry."

Cassie gasped. Certain that it wasn't her imagination. Those were Hayley's words in Hayley's voice, in her head. Finally, all their love came flooding back.

They were still connected; death couldn't sever their bond. She was right. Hayley had stayed as close as she could under the circumstances. And she had forgiven her. Cassie stared into the darkness. She was free to start again.

When this life was over, they would be together again, under better circumstances. Cassie wasn't going to break their pact of haunting this place together.

"I love you too Hayley. I didn't mean any of those things. I should have been there for you. I miss you so much. I wish you could know."

Cassie sat down with her back against the rock, she fumbled in her bag for a chocolate bar. A terrible hunger had crept up on her.

"Sweet sister, come closer. I need one last hug."

There was a tumbling of sound to her right, deeper within the tunnel behind her. Cassie swerved round unable to shine the light on it in time. Would it be possible to catch a glimpse of Hayley? To hug her one last time? What form did she take now? A pale ghost made beautiful in death or had green rot and purple decay got under her skin?

"Hayley?"

With the light shining down the tunnel she found a detail she hadn't noticed before, a squatting black mass darker than the shadows around it, was creeping closer and closer each time she looked away from it.

"Is that you Hayley?" If that was her, why was she being so shy?

"The light, it hurts me."

"No, Cassie, keep it on. Get out of here."

Which voice to follow? Someone was playing games with her in this dead place.

Hayley and Cassie weren't perfect, no relationship was, but despite their troubles and differences, Cassie knew her sister, inside and out.

It was Hayley that wanted a hug not the other interfering spirit.

"Ok, I'm turning it off."

The light clicked and the cold air around her plummeted, rushing against her with the force of a wave. Cassie waited in the silence. She got as far as counting to ten when she heard soft scrapings of something coming nearer, barely audible.

"I know you're there, Hayley."

"Turn it on, Cassie." The inside voice was stronger. Full of rage.

"You never listened to me."

There it was the cutting hurt that Cassie always inflicted upon her sister. She never meant to. She had only wanted what was best for her. It was her responsibility to try and help Hayley, only she could say the things that everyone else was thinking, that she was lazy, too morose, just needed to chill out and breathe.

That's all she ever wanted to do, help her sister become the best version she could be.

"Turn it on, now. If you want to live."

Cassie didn't want to risk scaring her sister away as she crawled closer, but something didn't feel right. She finished her chocolate bar, stuffing the wrapper hastily in her pocket. The crinkling sound echoed along each tunnel. She reached beside her for the torch.

Cassie couldn't find it. The torch wasn't where she left it. She whimpered as she swooped her hands over the floor. The ground was flat. It must have rolled away somehow, maybe she kicked it by accident?

It came rolling back into her hand.

When the light came back, the black mass was gone. It must have passed her. She shivered to think of the type of creatures that lived down here, these caves weren't as empty as people believed. The tunnels that ran under her town were teeming with dark matter. Cassie stood up, fighting the urge to run and hide, but how could she take cover where there was none to salvage? The darkness belonged to the monsters. She was trapped in the belly of a hungry beast.

Only one way to take now.

She turned around and peered down the tunnel. Maybe this way led back up? It was hard to concentrate on a route, not when there was the feeling that something other than her sister was watching close by. She headed the other way, wanting to be back up there sitting on the pew watching Garth watching her.

Her bones trembled. Something inside her was sending a warning. Maybe that thing hadn't gone away. In horror films nobody ever thinks to look above.

Slowly she raised her torch, higher and higher until its weak shivering glare was poised on the ceiling directly above her.

Nowhere left to look but up.

Something crouched above her head …

Chapter Thirty

Cassie

Present Day: March 20th, 9:00 p.m.

Cassie sucked in a breath of air along with dust, the ancient pagan magic, and the surrounding malice. Her mind froze. Unable to accept what her senses were communicating.

This.Can't.Be.Real.

Directly above her head, a monstrous thing hung upside down. Pale luminescent skin contrasting with dark oily liquid drooling from the beast's gaping mouth. Drip-by-warm-globular-drip onto Cassie's cheek marking the passage of long-drawn-out seconds.

Why couldn't she run? Cassie held her torch to her chest, hands locked together as if she was on her knees praying. Its fear had caught her. She couldn't trust anything down here, not even her legs to take her away.

This was no hallucination. Not this time. She wasn't tucked up in bed sweating out a nightmare. She was awake. She was in the caves. The creature staring down at her was real. The feeling on the back of Cassie's neck told her so. There was no way out.

She couldn't think. Standing in this spot she couldn't remember her past, the memories that could make her smile, not even the ones that made her cold, she couldn't contemplate the future. There was only what she could see. All she could do was observe as if from a distance, but nothing made sense here. This world had its own rules and laws of relativity. Dark replaced light, death ruled over life.

This thing looking down on her, moving its head all around as if deciding whether to swoop, had once been human but over time it had adapted to its environment. Didn't need the light anymore. Cassie was at a grave disadvantage. If this was what she was going to turn into she had no desire to survive.

What had caused it to become so mutated and bent out of shape? On first inspection it appeared more spider than bat. It's legs and arms so withered but strong and arachnid-like, but it hung upside down. Its grey hands and feet sprouting sharp overgrown talons, rooted deep into the soft chalk as if it were butter.

If she had wanted to, Cassie could have reached up and stroked the hide of the beast, thick and crinkled like an elephant's, forming deep dusty troughs and hillocks.

It didn't have the kind eyes of an elephant, only unblinking hungry black fisheyes focusing intently upon Cassie. Its gaze unwavering. What did it want?

How long had it been there? Had she gotten lost here unable to get out like Cassie? Did it have a loved one down here too which had kept it tethered?

Neither moved. Cassie hoped maybe if she stayed very still the creature would pass over. Maybe it hadn't seen her. Under these conditions there was a chance it could be blind. But wouldn't this darkness also deliver the creature extremely heightened senses?

When it tilted its head back, Cassie saw it was a small woman perched like a spider waiting in its web. Except this whole cave was her web with Cassie trapped inside. Running was futile. She'd seen the ease of that thing quickly scuttling towards her with its stick like limbs and talons.

The lips of the creature pulled back revealing blackened gums laced with drool and jutting piranha teeth partially hidden with rotten meat. It smiled malice down at her.

Cassie pushed herself back against the wall. Her breath fighting with her lungs.

A small growl resonated from the beast releasing a deathly stench unlike anything she had smelt before. Even more overpowering than being in that warm steaming bathroom with the scent of Hayley's spent coppery blood slowly heating her flat.

She didn't feel the sting on her arm at first. The creature moved fast. The thing held her glare whilst its arm swooped down at Cassie. It waited for her to blink.

Something hung from its claws. Like a coveted Christmas present it sniffed at it making soft cooing noises. It's prize, a thin translucent strip of peachy skin.

Her arm burned hot and cold.

The thing relaxed as it clambered down to inspect its bounty. It wasn't even looking at her, it had something else to play with. It didn't pay Cassie any further attention.

Cassie looked at her arm. The fabric of her hoodie torn asunder from those talons. Looking further in she saw the exposed glistening, sparkling flesh of her arm. An angry red line dotted with globules of blood that wasn't there before.

She looked back at the creature. That was hers. Cassie whimpered. That thing had her skin, played with it, enjoyed the feel of it in its wrinkled hands.

Cassie's arm shook. The wound was fizzing, cold fear spread upwards from her wound into her chest. If she wasn't careful, it would get infected.

The creature ate Cassie's ribbon of skin.

As it chewed it drew back, there was calm. It was satiated, the growling stopped. It must have been hungry. She prayed the ordeal was over. The creature had fed. It would move on and leave her alone. But instead, it climbed back up and looked down once more at Cassie. Hunger remained. It wanted more. Cassie was dinner, she had to get out of these caves. The only thing working in her favor was that it didn't like the torch Cassie held in her hands, now more powerful than a gun against the darkness.

Cassie took aim at its eyes.

The thing hissed, forced to scuttle back from the light of the torch, dirty doughy skin shriveling away from her. There was two meters of dark between them.

Still, it was reluctant to leave.

The creature stayed close hunting with a hungry lioness' determination prowling by a herd of grazing gazelle waiting for a weak spot. It wanted more of Cassie's soft young skin. The thing opened its mouth wide revealing the source of the darkness in the caves. This creature had created the darkness, it wasn't a natural absence of light.

There was no end to it.

Desperate sadness overwhelmed Cassie. Her life was futile. Her job was going nowhere, she had no friends. No one would notice her missing. Each day she lived was a day wasted. All she did was occupy her time. Passively living each day to the next until it was her turn to suffer and wane in old age, until she was no more.

Was this how Hayley felt for all those years? Suffering in silence because no one else understood. Somehow this creature had gotten to her. Had put her under its spell. Shown her the truth.

What had happened to Hayley in those moments when she'd disappeared in the caves by herself, the first time their parents had taken them to the caves? Cassie still remembered that day, they must have been ten years old. Cassie hadn't wanted to go. The day had been a hot one, she wanted to go to the park and meet her friends, but Hayley had jumped at the idea of going to the caves.

During the tour, Cassie had turned around and her sister had disappeared into the darkness. She'd hung back on purpose, but Hayley denied this when their parents went mad at her. How could she have been so stupid?

It had only been for a few moments but when she was returned to them covered in white chalk dust all over her jeans and scraped arms. A scratch on her cheek. She looked as if she had been missing for months rather than minutes.

Hayley had changed. There was a new look in her eyes, something only she could see. After that was when people began to call Hayley, Little Dolly Daydream, but they never questioned the sudden change in her. Cassie should have spoken up, should have made her parents see what she saw. That something had happened to Hayley in those lost minutes. She's come back diminished. Overnight she turned from an extrovert to an introvert, spending most of her time in her head with her own thoughts.

This creature took her sister away from her. The torch trembled with her hatred for the situation. Cassie couldn't stop looking at those sharp teeth congealed in black tar. The smell of rotten meat permeated the air and Cassie sealed her mouth against the rising taste of brackish water.

Cassie whimpered, frozen by the creature's strength. Not even bullets could be used against it.

It arched up growing evermore impatient, claws digging deeper. It screamed in frustration. Loose crumbs of rock crashed down. The sound made Cassie dizzy, she couldn't afford to lose her balance. Even if she so much as blinked...

Moving with the swiftness of a cat on its haunches, the creature backed up. Its intelligence made it more human than any other animal. Maybe it once was. Time had left no trace of humanity inside its heart.

"I told you. You should have listened. Now look at what has happened."

"I'm really sorry, Hayley," Cassie whispered struggling to find a steady rhythm of breathing. There wasn't enough air down here. Was it too late to pretend this wasn't happening?

The creature was waiting to feed. Cassie was the only living thing down here it could eat.

"Just keep the light on and get out of here."

"Which way should I go?"

"I don't know, I can't help you anymore."

"Just please, stay with me. I love you."

Cassie retreated backwards away from the stalking creature. Going back the way she came and although she'd never be able to retrace her steps at least she knew she was going in the right direction. Trouble was these tunnels wrapped around. They could be leading her further in. She stopped. What if there were more than one of those creatures scuttling behind her?

"Cassie!"

Something warm dripped onto her hair, she turned just in time. A screech turned her insides green. The light saved her. She needed to be vigilant if she was to get out alive.

It had been creeping towards her. It perched directly above her. Ready to strike. How could she have known when she was packing her bag in the safety of her bedroom what was calling her down here?

Did anyone else know about this beast? If she got out, she must warn people, would anyone believe her? Maybe she'd simply forget when she left the darkness?

It hardly mattered now. Getting out was a remote possibility such as being able to swim across the Atlantic. If she had a gun, she'd use it on herself.

Chapter Thirty-One

Cassie

Present Day: 20th March, 10:30 p.m.

When Cassie's torch went out for good, that would be it. Once the last flicker of light had been claimed by the darkness she would disappear too. The creature wanted her flesh.

She couldn't bear to think about seeing herself going into that slippery black mouth, piece by piece. Would she be savored slowly limbs first? How long would she have to watch herself slowly turn to bones and gristle?

Her belly filled with cold sloshing fear. Her remains would stay here for all eternity. She didn't want to imagine her own flesh turning cold, her skin turning waxen and grey, rotting down to dust. Entirely claimed by the creature. She would never be found.

Cassie came down here because she believed she could help her sister find peace. She wanted to put things right between them. She had been a fool. The light of day would never come, there was no sunrise of hope coming over the horizon, no new beginnings.

This was something she couldn't wait out. Only an endless darkness, a long cold lonely night that would never end.

She thought back to her previous lonely nights lying awake in bed, staring up at the ceiling going through an existential crisis realizing she was born to die. Piece by piece, Death was going to take her. Her life would amount to nothing. Those insomniac feelings of worthlessness and despair were nothing compared to this.

The creature perched above her.

Had anyone noticed her missing? When Hayley killed herself, her family broke apart. When Cassie left for university, her parents sold everything then moved to Spain. Putting distance between their guilt and their daughter's dead body. They had realized too late they'd let their little girl fall through the cracks.

Garth might have done but he was a good-looking fella, he was probably too inundated with female attention to come looking for her. They'd barely spoken. Cassie could picture him clearly in her mind. Yes, a guy like that, he would have forgotten all about her by now. She tried not to think of him. Another opportunity squandered.

Today, she'd come alone. Since her sister's death she kept herself to herself, refusing all offers of afterwork drinks and weekend meet ups with friends.

She's been missing for months.

No one was going to come.

Something inside shook. She jolted upright. What about the future that could have been hers? Surely that was worth fighting for. If she died now, she would never know what her life could have been like. What would happen to the children she wanted to have? Unless she survived this, they would never get born.

It was time to fight.

There was someone willing to fight for Cassie, herself. It was time to be her own best friend. Hayley was gone. She was never coming back. But Cassie was still here. For now, she was alive and what is life but surviving one moment to another?

Cassie must do this alone. She may be just one of billions of people on this planet, but she deserved a chance for a lifetime just like everyone else.

She had to rescue herself.

To get out, she must keep her torch focused on that thing and never look away from the nightmare slowly following her. Keep walking. Only the light keeps it back. *This is a game* she told herself, *I just need to hold my nerve steady like I'm holding the torch.*

Do or die.

All light died in the end. The creature was growing impatient, not used to being teased by its food, but it was willing to wait for those two little AA batteries to run out.

Judging by that thing's skin it was no servant to the passing of time. That creature was old, maybe even older than the caves. Cassie's two torches would only last for a few hours. What then?

Behind her came the movement of something else. Something walking on the floors, large stomping footsteps making no attempt to creep around undetected. The creature heard it too, hissing excitedly as it sniffed the air in big monstrous sounds.

Was it another creature? Was there going to be a fight over her flesh? They would tear her apart.

If only she could quickly find her way out of the Druid section and get back into the light where there were electric bulbs buzzing overhead, literally fizzing with light. She'd be safe. Surely the creature wouldn't follow her there?

The other thing approached.

Was it a tour group? Was she about to be rescued? Could these be her last seconds of torture? Should she scream help or hold herself quietly? Friend or foe?

She backed up faster, taking a risk.

Whatever it was, it walked on the floor, not on the ceiling. She could only hear one set of feet; no faint glow of lanterns or conversations being whispered far away.

Cassie dreamt of being up there again with the fresh air, the sounds of the living and soft glorious light that warmed the skin and heart. She'd do anything to witness a sunset.

Fuck it.

She turned and broke into a sprint, running faster and faster. It was still there following. It could run too. She needed precious distance between them.

How could something so old move so quickly?

A moment of distraction almost killed her. She ran into a pillar knocking her to the floor. Not where she wanted to be if she wanted to remain uneaten. She had to get back up and ignore her throbbing nose.

The torch rolled away from her reach. The light was still on, the filament intact. Cassie scrambled to reach it before the creature reached her.

As soon as it was back in her hand, she shone it above her. Her ankle had sustained some serious damage. Her muscles screamed with hot pain when she applied pressure. Pain that went down to the bone. She didn't think it was broken but she couldn't be sure. No looming creature above her, she sighed breaking out into tears. When would this living nightmare end? Maybe she should just get it over and done with and let it feed.

There was something standing near her, she felt the warmth. Whatever it was, it breathed. It lived.

A ghost stood before her; its face concealed with darkness. A young woman dressed in a thin white frock covering her entire length.

"Hayley?"

"Who the fuck are you?"

CHAPTER THIRTY-TWO

Sienna

Present Day: March 20th, 11:15 p.m.

This tunnel wouldn't end. It was supposed to have led her to safety, but it felt she was only going in one direction: down. She could feel bruises forming on her arms and legs. She had fallen countless times. There was no light to hold onto to help her out of this mess.

Just when she was starting to feel helpless, she saw a weak light in the distance. Hope grew in her chest but when she found someone else down here it didn't feel right.

For hours, Sienna had walked barefoot through tunnels leading nowhere. Silence accompanied her, so powerful it hummed around her. The darkness left her feeling like the last person alive, until this young woman came crashing into her.

"Hayley?"

"Who the fuck are you?"

She remained blank before suddenly turning around and coming back to look at Sienna. "Can you hear me? I'm Cassie."

"Obviously I can hear you. I'm standing right in front of you." Sienna wished this mad woman would stop prodding her.

"Oh," was all she said after a long pause.

Sienna remained unconvinced of this woman. She could be one of them. Sienna shuddered to think what they might have been planning to do to her.

Fiona's words haunted her still. *It's not about where you are, but where you're going young lady.*

The cost of her escape was a dead body to deal with. Fiona's son. She had to leave him there, no time to hide his remains. This time it had been self-defense.

She needed a new identity after this. Cassie was a nice name.

"Did Fiona send you down here?" Sienna slapped her hand away.

"Fiona? Is that her name?"

"Is Fiona down here?" Sienna looked past Cassie's shoulder but there was nothing. Would Fiona come down here looking for her?

In a carefully controlled whisper, "She was hanging from the ceiling." Cassie took another step, stroked Sienna's cheek. "You're real aren't you? Tell me you're real."

"I'm real." What a fuckwit. Why was she surprised that Sienna was alive? "Wait, did you say Fiona was hanging from the ceiling?"

"I saw her with my own eyes."

Sienna took hold of Cassie's arms and repeated her question. "Is Fiona working with you?"

Cassie winced in pain. "I don't know a Fiona."

"What about her half-baked son?" Sienna gripped her wrists harder until there was a pathetic whimper, this bitch wasn't hiding anything. She looked too stupid to be able to lie convincingly.

"Why are you here, all alone?"

"I was looking for someone, my sister." She began to cry.

Sienna let her go disgusted by her weakness. Cassie had come down here by her own choice. But she would know the way out.

"We need to get out of here," Cassie whispered.

That was one thing they could agree on. Sienna had already made up her mind to never trust anyone again after this day. She made sure to always keep Cassie in front as they walked through the tunnels.

Where she could see her at all times.

"Do you know where you're going?" Each tunnel looked the same to Sienna, there was no order to them, she felt like she was walking in circles. She couldn't take much more. It had been at least 24 hours since she had eaten or drunk water. There was so much dust making its way into her lungs, slowly choking her. It still felt like they were still going down. But she had to keep going.

"Keep up."

Sienna took orders from no-one.

None of this made any sense, later she would question it, figure it all out and serve up her revenge, but right now she was only concerned with getting out of these caves.

Being down here made her feel sick. The darkness filled every space as if it was a huge blob eating everything in its path. It felt like it was alive. If she didn't get out fast, she was going to end up mad like Cassie.

As if that wasn't enough for her to cope with, Sienna started seeing things flashes of light and strange faces watching her but unlike Cassie her mind was strong. Sienna focused on the light of the torch. The only real thing down here. She didn't believe in things she couldn't see, but it really felt like someone was following them. A young girl with the prettiest smile who kept calling her name, her real name, Melanie.

But of course, Maura couldn't be down here. She was dead and buried in the little churchyard back home.

The only way out is ahead, she told herself. Sienna kept her eyes up front and carried on. It was like walking on the moon. Or maybe it was like being at the bottom of the ocean. The very bottom of the world.

"I was kidnapped by the way, thanks for asking." Sienna looked across at Cassie, of all the people to be trapped down here with.

Trying to have a conversation with Cassie was as productive as having a conversation with a toaster. No response. Absolutely nothing.

"They put me in a cage, took all my clothes. They were going to kill me. But I escaped. I killed one but the other one, the woman, is still up there. Soon, she'll come looking for me." Her voice trailed off.

Cassie had no interest at all in what had been done to Sienna. She wasn't even listening.

Only her torch was of interest.

Cassie was consumed with needing to constantly scour the walls with pale torch light, searching for an exit. Their journey was taking too long because of it, and that torch was on its last legs. She couldn't shake off the feeling someone was behind them. If anyone knew the caves well, it would be Fiona.

It was hard to see where they were going, whether it was a wall or more black air in front of them. Cassie kept insisting on shining the torch on the ceiling which was of no use to anyone. She wouldn't let Sienna anywhere near the torch.

It unnerved Sienna that this girl was here by herself. Had she escaped from somewhere too? Or had she had chosen to put herself in this situation? Wanting to be here.

"Are you hot? It's so hot down here. I feel like I'm covered in ants." Cassie took off her hoodie as if it was on fire and stuffed it in her rucksack. "I'm really warm." There was an edge to her voice.

Cassie was holding something back. She was showing some strange injuries on her arms.

Sienna rubbed her bandaged arm. She was good at reading people, it's what got her through life. Cassie had no interest in Sienna, she didn't want to talk. All she talked about was getting out. So far, they both wanted the same thing. It made sense to stay together for a little longer.

"Why are you down here?" Sienna stepped up closer, rubbing her arms to generate much needed body heat, hoping Cassie might get the hint.

"Oh, it's a long story. I became separated from my group. They do tours here."

This hellhole was a tourist attraction? There was a way out somewhere except Cassie couldn't remember where it was.

"The only thing to be concerned with is finding our way back to the light. That's what will save us. We must never stop looking."

Sienna nodded. That was all she needed to know. Cassie was a fruit basket. She looked behind her quickly in the direction of an approaching sound and walked straight into Cassie's back. They both jumped quickly before carrying on.

Cassie had a rucksack, there was some semblance of intelligence in that little cotton head. What else was in there apart from that nice warm hoodie?

Sienna couldn't help but hate Cassie. Who wouldn't? An attractive middle-class girl who spoke well, wore expensive branded clothes, and led a charmed life. She'd had everything handed to her.

She would never know what it was like for people like Sienna who needed to do terrible things to people who had a lot, to have the lifestyle she deserved. People like Cassie would never know what it meant to be alive.

"What's in the bag Cassie?" Where was that hoodie she took off?

Before Cassie had a chance to turn and respond, Sienna was unhooking it off her back and opening it.

"Help yourself." Cassie replied eager to get going again. "There's not much in the way of food I'm afraid."

Cassie didn't make a fuss; they were a team, she was glad to have someone with her. She only cared about having a torch in her hands, shining it as if she was hunting for a lost engagement ring, swinging wildly in a blind panic to illuminate every part of the darkness.

Cassie waited, whilst Sienna looked in the bag. Beads of sweat gathered on her brows and dripped along her cheeks. She really was burning up. She better not collapse; Sienna wasn't going to carry her.

Inside Cassie's rucksack was a bottle of water, which she drank before Cassie could protest. There was a torch, pants, jogging bottoms, and a warm cozy jumper.

Cassie dived in taking the second torch before Sienna had a chance to discover it and hid it away in her back pocket.

Cassie wasn't lost. She had planned this out. Why? Just how long was this crazy bitch planning on staying down here? Sienna fished out two chocolate bars and ate them in a frenzied attack.

"That's an unusual dress you're wearing."

Sienna scowled. "It's what those freaks put me in." Sienna spoke more harshly than she needed to. After all Cassie was helping her, proving her worth by letting her take the spare clothes but how could she have forgotten Sienna's dire situation?

People were trying to kill her. What if they caught her again?

"Don't worry about them, they won't hurt you down here, just worry about getting out." Cassie waited as Sienna got changed. Still shining her torch.

"Do you mind?" Sienna said, again in a voice too harsh, but it was how she survived. You have a license to be a bitch when you have nothing else.

"I was checking if there's anything behind us."

Cassie carried on, eager to see what waited at the end of their tunnel. It was getting wider and taller. That must be good right?

Sienna punched her limbs through, dressing quickly. She was completely naked under this flimsy see-through cotton shift dress. She couldn't be dressed like that when she was back on the streets of London.

"Why would there be anything behind us?" Sienna narrowed her eyes, either Cassie was hiding something big from her or she was bat shit crazy.

"Just want to be sure we're not being followed," Cassie replied.

Sienna knew there was something she wasn't telling her, but she let it go, Cassie was being useful. Nobody stood a chance trying to sneak up on Sienna. She'd been here before if anyone could lead them out it was her.

"Hey Cassie, I think before we head up, we need to get our stories straight."

"Oh? Why?"

"Well, if you've gone missing as you say ..." Sienna paused giving Cassie a moment to come clean, which she didn't. "There's going to be a lot of people looking for you, police, fire crew maybe even an ambulance on standby. The media could be involved. This is a very big newsworthy story, Cassie. What are you going to say to explain yourself when they find you?"

"The truth, I got lost."

"The truth? No, you've got to think smart. Can you do that? Think on your feet?"

"I don't know what you mean." Cassie stopped searching the narrow tunnel they were in. "Am I in trouble?"

"Big time. You'll be charged for their time, and it won't come cheap. Plus, the media will destroy you. Do you want to see your face on the *Daily Mail's* front page claiming what a moron you are? They'll come after your family too." Sienna ripped up the dress, letting it fall to the floor. "But I can help, seeing as you've let me borrow these clothes, how about I pretend to be you? I'll say you came down to find me. I'll be Cassie and you can be Sienna. A new life, a new start."

Cassie grinned. "Would you do that for me?"

"Yeah."

Fool, Sienna smiled before remembering who she was now. No longer was she Sienna but Cassie.

Now she was going to be a nice young girl, well, until she got away from here

Thank God for the darkness hiding her real self.

Cassie walked on, her sense of entitlement her downfall. She expected Sienna to clean up her mess, and not even a thank-you.

"Melanie, I want you to play with me." The voice now sounded like it was right behind them.

Sienna grabbed Cassie. "Did you hear that?"

Cassie shrugged. "Don't let the darkness get to you, trust me. Look, let's take this right turn."

CHAPTER THIRTY-THREE

Bill

Present Day: March 21st, 00:15 a.m.

As Bill entered a tunnel, he heard screaming.

It meant only one thing. He was too late. The cries were close by near the Druid's Altar. Bill guessed they were no more than thirty meters away. Bill held his torch a little tighter; that thing, the White Lady was close by too. The matter was unfortunately closed. Cassie hadn't deserved to die like that, to have your heart eaten in front of you as the world turned black for good.

Bill had done all he could without getting into more trouble with Fiona but on this occasion it wasn't enough. Next would be that awful conversation he'd need to have with Garth. He rubbed the back of his head. What on earth was he going to do about Garth? He really hoped Garth had taken his advice and fled.

He had no reason to stay any longer. They would have to wait it out. Poor girl. She'd suffer forever down here. By morning her face would be carved onto the walls with all the other faces.

Garth was his priority now. He needed to go back up and ensure his safety. He turned full circle with his torch.

"Damn," he muttered to himself. He was in the Druid section. Not far from the altar. He shivered as goosebumps rippled over his skin. He wanted to get out of here as quickly as possible. That poor young girl. Garth had seemed very concerned for Cassie. He had no idea what to tell him.

They wouldn't find the body.

No one would.

The White Lady had her own places in these caves, clandestine dwellings where no mortal returns from. Bill has suspected over the years that there must be a lair down here, another underground set of tunnels running adjacent to the ones he walked.

Fiona only told him the bare minimum. His job was to make sure the White Lady was never discovered. He was Fiona's eyes and ears when she wasn't here. To keep everything running smoothly and to make sure none of the tourists got eaten.

When he asked too many questions, she would serve him that lingering death stare and tell him to mind his business. It always set his pulse racing. Fiona knew an awful lot on dark magic. After all these years, after everything she'd put him through, the captivity she kept him in, she still treated him like an outsider.

He'd heard some strange things when he'd been alone down here; lost noises of the eternally suffering entombed in a dark cold place trying to get back in, wailing eternally when they realize they can't re-enter the world of the living.

Bill had always feared his own death. At his age, he thought about it all the time. It wasn't the thought of endless oblivion but that there was an existence beyond death. Not living just eternal pain, the endless suffering that the White Lady took relish in. She tended to this endless suffering as if it were her garden, and the lost souls her coveted blooming perennial flowers.

This home of hers, these dark endless caves. This was a realm of the dead. Where they went after their last breath. It would explain the unusual abundance of ghosts. They must be the lucky ones, half in half out.

Somewhere hidden in the dark there must be a gap between the underworld and his world on the surface. There was so much about the caves still to be discovered. Mysteries he would never know. All his adult life he's been used as a pawn by Fiona. How he hated this place. But he could never leave. Not even in death. Tomorrow he would have to show up for work like nothing had happened. He'd have to put on that smile on all day, crack some killer one-liners, and play his part as an old eccentric tour guide for the visitors who'd arrive tomorrow for their underground tours. Every day of his life always the same.

"Fuck!" he screamed with rage that fuels a Viking running into battle. He kicked the walls, almost threw his torch in anger but rescued himself just in time. In the distance he heard running. The White Lady had heard him, she must still be on the prowl. Even he was scared at the thought of running into her.

He turned left and walked as fast as he could without making a sound. Kept his breathing quiet too. No point in everyone having to die tonight. He had spares but torches were worth more than gold down here. There was a good whisky in the kitchen hidden behind the microwave, he'd earnt himself a big drink. He'd need something for the nerves. Help him plan for the loose ends in this situation. There was Fiona to deal with.

Garth.

What could be done about him? Bill knew already he'd come back to the caves. Fiona wanted him dealt with, but he couldn't kill him. Bill couldn't do that to Sandra. He wouldn't take away her beloved son. He must protect Garth at all costs.

There must be another option. Was it time to come clean about the caves? How much should Garth know? He didn't want him involved in this any longer. He had to say enough to scare the shit out of him. Make sure he never returned.

Bill had some money saved up. He'd never had any holidays. He would hand it over, tell him to run. Garth needed to know what would happen if he didn't leave. Fiona never forgets. Never leaves matters unfinished.

Near the front of his tunnel, he heard laughter. A very common ghost manifestation down here. It was a good sign. The White Lady must be far away. Not even the ghosts liked her.

He walked towards the noise, it was only when he was thirty feet away could he make out a conversation. It wasn't the sound of ghosts conversing to one another, but of two young women.

Both very much alive, and uneaten.

He saw them in silhouette forms. When they realized he was standing there watching them, they erupted in fear screaming deep into the darkness. But he wasn't the big bad wolf.

It was dangerous to scream.

He ran towards them. He only had a few moments to act. He had to make them calm and quiet. But he was easily twice their size. He saw the whites of their eyes widening as they screamed at his approach. Nothing apart from getting them out of the caves would calm them down.

A short woman with long brown hair even went as far as to try and strike him when he attempted to put his arms around her.

The first strike came at him, sharp nails ready to rip off his face. He was ready, easily catching her fist in one grab. He forced her arm back down into submission.

"Who are you?" Sienna hissed. A young woman cowered behind her.

"I'm Bill, I work here," he whispered, then raised his finger to his lips for quiet. He looked behind them and then over his shoulder. He couldn't see anything approaching them unawares, but this was no time to relax. They had to get out.

The White Lady would have heard them. She would now know exactly where they were. If she found three people, she'd eat three people.

"Do you know the way out?"

Bill looked at the other young woman who had spoken. How could there be two of them? Garth said there had only been one. He said her name was Cassie. Garth had lost two people?

"Yes, I can show you the way out." But first he needed to find out which one was Cassie.

The only one who mattered.

The woman who had just tried to hit him stepped forward. This time she was composed. She held out her hand to shake Bill's.

"You must be the rescue party, I'm Cassie." She stepped aside to let him see the younger girl reluctant to look at him. "This is

Sienna. I know this sounds crazy, but you must believe us. Sienna was kidnapped and she'd been held by a mad old witch, but she managed to escape into these tunnels. We desperately need your help to get out before the witch comes back. We're so frightened."

"I see," Bill looked down at the woman with curly hair claiming to be Sienna. *So very young*, he thought, usually the chosen are much older with a lifetime of crimes to be absolved from. Fiona had a list of people she had been watching for many years. This Sienna must have done something utterly despicable she looked so sweet and harmless.

She was the chosen sacrifice for the creature. Sienna took a step forward, she was about to hug him, but Bill was forced to push her back, her eyes full of hurt and fear.

"I was looking for my sister." She tried to grab hold of him again. He shoved her backwards. This was the woman who had drowned her own baby sister.

He couldn't go against Fiona. He particularly did not want to anger The White Lady. Why was it always him that had to do the dirty work around here?

"I'm only bringing one of you up." He held out his arm to keep Sienna at bay.

The girl claiming to be Sienna was very confused. She raised her hands in protest, her eyes open wide. "Hang on, wait a minute, no, this can't be right. You can't leave me down here with that thing. I've seen it. Look it scratched me on my arm. It was a mistake. I'm sorry for what I did but I've learned my lesson. I won't wander off again. I've spoken to my sister, it's fine now."

"She forgave you?" Bill rubbed his beard. "None of that matters." He backed away. "If it's seen you, it's too late."

Bill pulled the first woman away, she dutifully followed with a smirk, eager to be at his side. "It's not up to me, you don't know who you're messing with," he said with regret.

"But I'm Cassie," Cassie screamed. "I'm the real Cassie."

"She's lying," replied Sienna, hanging on the crook of Bill's arm, she smacked the torch out of Cassie's hands.

Cassie screamed and scrambled around on all fours in the dirt for her torch.

In the chaos, Sienna and Bill ran off, glad to be going back up. Shame rippled through him. He had condemned Sienna to die. The other young woman ran on ahead. He was sure he heard her laughing to herself. *Right, that's it,* he thought. *I'm not doing this anymore.*

CHAPTER THIRTY-FOUR

Garth

Present Day: March 21st, 00:45 a.m.

The surrounding cold slowly seeped into his body, and the darkness drained him, filling his mind with fear. The silence of the caves was a most terrible companion.

Even a raging introvert who clung to solitude like a life jacket in an angry ocean would have craved company under these conditions. This was his nightmare, he had no one to help him bear the burden of trying to save Cassie's life.

Going down, he'd had grand dreams of becoming a hero and rescuing his girl, carrying her out in his arms to a tremendous applause, maybe even finding that lost part of himself.

It was time to see sense. He'd been here a long time. If he had been on a trek, he would have reached his destination by now. He hadn't found her. Cassie was gone. His mind went over the last moments when he'd seen her. Something didn't make sense.

His was still struggling to understand how he had lost someone. He'd done everything right. Just as he had been trained, he kept a constant headcount of his group to make sure no one had wandered off. But she had.

How? Why?

Despite his current surroundings, and the realization he too was very lost, he couldn't stop thinking about her. Didn't want to believe he might never see her again.

He wanted desperately to see her again. To know that she was safe.

Garth had only known Bill for a short time but that didn't stop him from looking up to him. He thought to himself. What would Bill do in this situation? Of course, Bill would never find himself in this predicament. He was a levelheaded man who took everything in his stride. Nothing got the better of him, not even these caves. He always knew what to do in every situation. How he wished he was like Bill.

With no one to talk to down here he imagined bumping into Bill, the beacon of sensibility. What would Bill be saying to him if he were here now? He wiped hot tears from the back of his hand.

Bill would start off by stroking is long white beard, slip his fingers in the belt of his jeans and look him in the eyes then shake his head.

"You did all you could boy, but you can't find her. It's time to come back up."

"I don't want to leave her down here."

"There are things you don't know about this place. She's gone. Don't let this ruin the rest of your life. You're still young and free."

Garth nodded to himself as the image of Bill standing before him drifting away as quickly as clouds on a windy day.

Should he go back up? Do what he should have done hours ago call the police and hand himself in? The caves needed to be searched properly not by an idiot with a torch.

Garth shone his torch both ways, the air surrounding him was murky like dirty ocean water mixed with silt and sludge. Everything down here was so hopeless. Silence made his ears ring. What else could he do? He stood up and straightened his shoulders, resolving to go back up and get outside help.

He shouldn't be alone. Nor should she be here all alone. He had to get out of this darkness, it was pressing against him like dead cold bodies in a mass grave pit. Everything was so cold, so bleak. Garth tripped and turned a corner, the tunnel came to dead end. His knees fell onto sharp flint scattered on the rough floor surface. Excavation had been abandoned hundreds of years ago. He rubbed grit from his palms, he'd never found a dead end before. How far was he from the entrance? No one knew for sure how far these caves went.

No way out.

Garth began to cry, at least no one could see down here. The darkness helped him accept the failure that he was. He couldn't help Cassie any more than he could help himself. He'd let her down so badly.

His back ached, pain fired along his legs with each step as he set off. He took a right this time, then another one. Maybe if he just kept turning in one direction only, he could find his way out? His hands stung from a biting coldness. The damp soaked into his jeans, his skin was clammy cold underneath. He turned another corner, he was back where he had started.

The flare was dying out.

The creature would come back soon. His heart began to beat faster urging him on. Why was it so hard to make any progress down here?

Was she still around, waiting in the shadows just out of sight? Watching him cry? He couldn't sense anything near him, but his senses were useless down here. This was not a fair battle against a creature who could see in the dark, scuttle over all surfaces and move like a bear trap clamping shut.

Time to get moving.

He needed to leave.

Sitting here Garth was as accessible as a plate of food. He knew these caves like no other, was confident he could find his way back. At least up above where the air was fresh and sweet, things would be better, though not by much.

He was responsible for this mess. He should have been the one to have called the police, let the authorities know when there was a chance something could have been done about it.

If she was never found, it would be all on him. He should have called the police straightaway. He could go to jail for this. He should.

He rested against a wall. His hands reached out to ease the strain.

Instead of meeting cold rock he fell through the air. He landed in a gap between the walls. His knee exploded in pain but what he saw took his breath away. A clever illusion that kept the entrance hidden, clearly man made. He had slipped through a gap leading to a secret passage.

Too tired to think, he followed.

Stone steps lead down into a huge cavern.

"This can't be happening." His voice echoed around him bouncing off the walls. For a moment he thought he'd found another living soul. But no, still just him.

He followed them down into a huge cavern shaped in a church. The high vaulted ceilings reminded him how deep he was. In the center was a large wooden table, round not square. Eight places set with dull metal chalices and wooden plates hidden neath a veil of cobwebs and dust. He shone his torch to see more. In the center was a handful of jewelry. A few rings and a necklace. They were modern, he inspected the necklace, it had come from Pandora, a modern brand.

This was a chamber. A dwelling.

Now he knew the reason why no one was permitted to venture off the designated tour route. *This* is what must stay hidden. Now he had his first answer. This was why archeological investigations weren't allowed below the surface.

Who knew this was here? Everyone, apart from him?

In the far corner of the chamber, there was a little pool collecting rainwater drip by drip, the water surprisingly clear. He was thirsty but he didn't drink.

Piles of shining jewels set in brooches, rings and torcs sparkled as his torch found them nestled into the rock crevices like mussels huddled together when the tide is out. This must have been centuries and centuries of offerings. His eyes skimmed over bronze coins, stone carvings of a beautiful woman the color of moonlight. The rock floor beneath him was worn smooth to marble.

Despite all the grandeur, there was an unearthly stench mixed in with the damp. It was coming from the walls. He made his way over, careful not to tread on anything. The walls stretched up high. There must be houses above this. People had no idea what lay beneath them.

Row upon row of shelves were cut into the walls. Each one filled with skulls. Some were so old they had turned brown. Big black pits for eyes stared out into the eternal darkness, the paler more recent ones collected at the front. So many skulls. Thousands at least. Was one of them Cassie's? He shuddered and looked away.

The perfect home for someone who hated light.

This is where *she* lives.

But if she wasn't here, where was she? Would she come back soon with Cassie's bitten-off head dripping in her jaws?

Moving back to the entrance he found books, huge tomes of lost knowledge. Would they disintegrate in his hands if touched? He reached out. What was in these books? Lost history of the Druids? Spells? The secret to eternal life?

Now wasn't the time. He felt in his back pocket for his phone. It was long gone. He had no hope of finding it so he could take photos of his discovery. Even if there was phone reception down here, ho could no longer call for help.

He needed to live.

If he survived this, he'd return. But he wouldn't come alone. He trusted Bill, together they would look through this place. *Bill's a good guy*, he thought, *I hope he's not in danger*. If only his dad had been more like Bill.

He retraced his steps backwards coming to the dark wooden table in the center.

There he saw a dagger the length of his forearm. It was heavy. He lifted it to the light to see better. It was a fine thing; the handle was of Celtic swirls and patterns. The blade shone, still as sharp as the day it was forged. He knew in these sorts of situations it's forbidden to take anything from ancient abodes like these, but having this dagger made him feel a little less scared.

Beside the dagger was a chalice with a dark liquid inside. When he held it, there was warmth in his hands. He held his face away, hoped it wasn't blood. He took a tentative whiff holding it at arm's length.

"Coffee?"

Someone had been down here recently.

CHAPTER THIRTY-FIVE

Cassie

Present Day, March 21st, 1:15 a.m.

They had left her behind. Alone, again, plunged into darkness.

Why wouldn't Bill take me with him?

The floor beneath her thrummed. Something was coming towards her.

"Sienna, Bill?" she hissed, keeping herself down low. She hadn't seen which way they had gone. The only way that would lead to the surface. Without that man to guide them, she would never know.

The darkness pressed in on her, wrapping her in a dark cocoon. The darkness began to feed on her. Why did it feel so constrictive, was it choking her? Her torch, she must find her torch.

There was no need for Sienna to have thrown it so hard. Was her name even Sienna or was that another lie? Why had she been so quick to place her trust in a stranger?

Especially one who was walking here alone.

On her hands and knees, Cassie searched the floor sweeping her hands in wide circles. Slicing them open with grit and flint did not hamper her efforts.

The torch had to be found—else she'd die. Shuffling to her right, she eventually found something that wasn't rock and grabbed hard. Her torch. It rattled in her hands. The torch hadn't rattled before.

"No, no no, please."

She flipped the switch back and forth. Hot tears of molten fear dripped down her cheeks, her thumb clicking painfully with the force.

It would not give her light. She tried ten times more, trying to see if there was a way, hoping she could coax it as she would a stubborn car engine that doesn't want to run on a cold wet morning.

No matter how fast she flipped it on, hurting the joints in her fingers with so much force, nothing worked. Not even a gentle easing motion. She reached into her backpack.

The second torch. It was gone.

"That bitch!"

Had Sienna taken it too? There was no other torch. No other lifeline. Well, that was it then. Were these going to be her final hours? Or minutes?

She must stay very quiet and hope the creature had lost the scent of her blood. Behind her, she heard noises. Of rock being picked out of its niche, tumbling down.

Cassie trembled. What direction was best to take? What was she supposed to do now? She hated the feeling of being alone down here.

From nearby came a heavy scuttling sound of thin hard spindly legs rapping in a long succession over soft ground, a sound a giant spider could make, each of its eight furry spiky legs tapping its steely way all over the walls paying no heed to gravity. A spider that could move fast. A spider who wanted to eat.

It was coming for her.

Cassie didn't cry at the thought of being left on her own with the creature. She didn't wonder who that man was and why he so steadfastly refused to take her back up with Sienna. Bill seemed to know what else was down there. He was a big guy; possibly ex-military, age had had no impact on his strength, but he was scared.

No, she didn't think of any of those things. She just ran.

Answers are futile without light at the end of the tunnel. Her legs weren't used to running, but she pushed them as fast as they would go. She kept her arms outstretched to feel for walls and corners. The fever had really taken hold of her, making her mind feel fuzzy and her clothes damp. The exploding pain of blood expanding through tiny blood vessels were a comfort to her, anything that reminded her she wasn't dead. Not yet.

Her legs expanded further filling with lactic acid. A stitch the size of a hot-water bottle took hold of her right-hand side. She clutched it but refused to slow her pace. The pain felt like tiny spider creatures scratching away her innards to get out and be reunited with their dark infested mother. Her chest heaved, her throat dried. There wasn't enough air down here.

This place wasn't intended for human survival, it's only for the end.

How long did these caves go on for? How far could she run until it caught up? Garth had said it went on for over twenty-two miles, that only a small section of the caves had been properly explored. How could it possibly stretch that far? Was she going to have to run forever?

Until she reached her grave? Her own little spot in this darkness.

The drum of her blood rushing blocked out all other noises. She had no idea if that thing was close behind her. It was coming, sooner or later Death comes for us all. She didn't want to know when it would strike. She was powerless against those sharp black claws and teeth. It was going to eat her sliver by sliver.

Nothing could escape those black marble eyes.

"Keep going Cassie." Her sister was waiting for her.

There was hope in Hayley's voice.

Cassie wouldn't be completely alone in the darkness. Would that existence be better than complete oblivion?

Even if she made it out, she'd never be the same again, she'd changed, seen beyond what a mortal mind should see.

There was so much she wanted to do. Cassie was twenty-three, she hadn't even started her life yet. Nothing had begun. Why had she wasted her small portion?

There was Garth, up there. Why didn't she carry on following him through the darkness and back up into the light?

She pictured them sharing a drink in a dimly lit pub after saying yes to him, his eyes creased from smiling, giving her shy looks when she talked, both growing tipsy and intoxicated together. Who knew where that could have led?

Instead, she was down here.

She turned a corner and saw something up ahead. It started as a deep mist with a hint of red, like the hot core of the earth, there was a smell of smoke, but it wasn't a fire.

There was light ahead.

It was a trap laid out for her, but just to see a little light before she was killed would be some measure of salvation.

The colors grew in vibrancy, reaching out with hazy tendrils to greet her and take her into its embrace that was neither cold nor warm.

She ran to it.

There was a slim chance this could somehow be her way out. Was it light from up above? Had they opened the wide doors? Could she get there before they sealed them?

Within the center of the red mist, she saw a figure crawling out of the wall.

"Cassie?"

"Garth? Tell me that it's really you? Don't say I'm imagining it"

"It's me." He held out his arms.

She beamed. Garth had come back. For her.

CHAPTER THIRTY-SIX

Garth

Present Day: March 21st, 1:20 a.m.

They collided into an embrace.

"Garth, I don't believe it. You came back, for me?"

Garth had never seen someone other than his mum look so pleased to see him. She held out her trembling arms. Tears gathered in her dark thick eyelashes. He wanted to tell Cassie all about the underground lair, but he held back. She probably just wanted to get out.

Unless it was her lair, and she was going to drag him back down there. Except seeing Cassie again made Garth certain that she didn't look like the sort to harbor a secret that dark; though he kept his distance just in case.

They both tried to speak at the same time and stopped, spoke again, and stopped. Until Garth squeezed her shoulders.

"Let's get out of here," she pleaded, with the biggest eyes he'd ever seen. "There's something down here," she whispered moving her eyes to the dwindling flare. "How long until this goes out? I don't have a torch."

"Here." He fished one out for her, his Turbo 500, feeling like a man for the first time in his life.

"I'm sorry Garth. I had to see my sister. She's here, with the dead." She hugged the torch close to her and quickly switched it on showering herself in light.

Garth nodded, she wasn't making any sense, he needed her to stay calm.

"I'm so glad I found you. I know the way out."

"Garth, I could kiss you."

"Could you?"

He turned to face Cassie. This is all he has ever wanted.

She walked over to him, getting closer and closer. Her hair smelling of honey, the curls felt so soft as he wrapped them around his fingers. She looked at him in total love and trust.

He leaned in, ready to close his eyes.

Cassie's eyes opened wide with white horror. Garth felt a rush of air coming at him. There was no time to look around.

The creature came without warning. It leapt on Garth's back, scratching at his skin trying to find a way in through his clothes and backpack to his soft flesh.

"Not today, Satan. Not today."

Garth was quick. He pulled out the dagger he'd borrowed from the lost chamber and struck at the devil on his back. Hard crust gave way in brittle chips. Rank oily black blood began to ooze down his left leg. There was no time to stop. Behind him the thing growled in pain as its grip on his rucksack loosened.

Garth threw the creature off, he twisted away from it as it fell to the floor with a loud thud. The light had weakened it. He stood proudly with his hands on his hips. *Not all heroes wear capes*, he mused.

The creature writhed in pain, her sharp talons clutched her belly shut but still her insides slipped out. Garth had cut her open. He felt weightless. His father now a distant memory. He tried to picture his dad's angry face but couldn't.

"Garth!" Cassie dragged him away. Black oil and viscera puddled on the floor. He hadn't done enough.

The creature was preparing to get back up.

Cassie ran in to the fight. With no weapon other than fear and fury she kicked the thing screaming out hot anger each time.

"You killed my sister. You took her from me."

Garth leant back in, stabbing it in the chest. It was hard work, but they couldn't leave until they were sure it was dead. It would never leave them alone if it was allowed to live.

"It won't die," he cried with weakness.

"Give it to me." Cassie took the dagger from him, clambered on top of the beast with both hands raised she plunged down.

Anger took control. Garth watched Cassie reduced to primal rage. After being down here he knew how it felt. Her brain would be telling her to attack, wrench out the blade, repeat. Nothing else mattered.

The creature hissed underneath her. Cassie found a spot underneath the thing's ribcage where the flesh finally yielded. The creature screamed.

"This will be your home now," the creature rasped as it's sharp talons tore at Cassie's clothes.

"I hate you," Cassie screamed. She didn't falter in her attack. Her arm felt like it was going to fall off but just one moment of rest would get her killed.

Garth smiled when he heard wet gloopy sounds. Even still Cassie carried on, she was taking no chances.

There was a long hiss as a black mist stirred up around them. The cave became lighter, the darkness retreated. Cassie's hair blew in her face, she swatted it away and saw the thing underneath: the creature rendered into a deflating husk of dried flesh and bone.

The deed was done.

Garth and Cassie watched on, holding hands. All that remained was grey dust. The darkness took the remains absorbing it back into the walls. Cassie collapsed to the floor.

Finally, they were alone.

"It's over," Garth whispered squeezing tight Cassie's hand.

CHAPTER THIRTY-SEVEN

The Dark Before the Dawn

Present Day: March 21st, 1:20 a.m.

It was time. The darkness was ready to eat mortal flesh.

The ritual was ready to begin.

Gerry, her son, was nowhere to be seen. Fiona had known he had snuck back in to be with Sienna. It was about time he took an interest in the opposite sex. She would find another for him. The White Lady had Cassie to feast upon.

This one, Sienna, was now hers.

There was also that young man Garth to deal with. She would ensure he would never speak to anyone of Cassie going missing. It wouldn't be hard to lure him into her home and deal with him too.

Fiona was in her bedroom sorting through her beloved vintage dresses. It had been an age since she had worn them. How she longed to dance again with a man on her arm. *Soon,* she promised herself.

The foundations of her house shook with fury, the portraits rattled against the walls, the floors shuddered and the chandelier in the hallway tinkled in fear. Down below a storm was raging through every dark turn and shadow. The darkness was screaming. It had never screamed before. Something wasn't right.

Was her mistress not satisfied with Cassie? Was she making her way up here to feast on every living soul she could find until the sun rose?

Fiona hobbled down the stairs, her knees grinding with each step she took. She staggered to her mirror. Hot, flustered, and helpless she watched herself age in quick time. A few hours ago, her hair was sleek and lustrous. But as she stood, it turned dull and began to thin. When she took a strand between her thumb and index finger it felt like dry tinder. Her posture began to curve and stoop, her balance uneven. Around her ankles was a black mist seeping out from the caves. The darkness was escaping, her mistress was no longer holding back out of sight.

Fiona needed to feed before she could figure out what to do next. She hobbled to the secret passageway leading to the cellar. She needed another slice of Sienna. The door was still locked but when she stepped inside, the room was empty.

On the other side of the door was her son, his head entirely caved into a mush of red clots and white brain jelly.

"Oh, my sweet boy."

Fiona did not say goodbye, her eyes scanned the room.

"No!" Fiona banged her fists limply on the table. Sienna was gone. The door leading down to the caves open.

Sienna was supposed to be hers, but she had escaped. Twice. Her fury turned to calm. She turned slowly to the remains of her son and howled. There was no choice. She needed to feed.

All was not lost, Fiona would still have her revenge.

She locked both doors behind her. There was no way out for Sienna. She would never see the sun again nor breath in sweet fresh air. Best of all Fiona would see it all by watching in her black mirror.

***

The shaking continued. Bill and Sienna both noticed the darkness had changed. Lifting like dawn fog burning up in the early morning sun. The weight of it was lighter. Above them they could see shafts of moonlight when moments before they had been absent.

"What's happening?" Sienna grabbed Bill's arm to stop him from running away.

"The darkness, its changing." He felt a sharp pain in his chest. His heart shuddering like a frightened animal.

They were so close to the exit. Finally, they were both running uphill gaining momentum. The path was of concrete, there was buzzing lighting overhead.

Something wasn't right.

"Help me." Bill reached up for Sienna's hand. He missed and stumbled to the floor, clutching his chest, struggling to breathe.

She remained unmoved looking down on him with disgust. "I think I can find my own way out from here."

"You're not Cassie, are you? She wouldn't leave me to die here."

Sienna laughed as she kicked his outstretched hand away.

***

"Here we are Cass," Garth pointed to one of the hidden exits leading out of the caves. "We've made it." He grabbed her hands, but she withdrew from the onslaught of moonlight.

He wanted so badly to run out, but he waited for her. In the moonlight the darkness around them didn't seem so bad. He couldn't keep the grin off his face. Somehow, they had made it out. They were survivors. He was going to stay awake and crack open a beer to toast the imminent sunrise. What a day this had been, thankfully it was over.

Now started the rest of his life. He found a star to swear by, he was never going to lose her again.

"Hurry up Cassie."

She wouldn't follow him to where he stood in the light. He had climbed up the verge and stood on a quiet country road. Breathing in the freshest air he had ever tasted. The night lay gentle around him. In the distance was the sound of traffic. There were streetlights ahead. He was only a ten-minute walk from home.

"It's so beautiful." He looked up at the moon.

Cassie looked very pale, almost luminescent. There was horror in her eyes. One of her arms was outstretched, entwined with a pale form beside her. It resembled a dark mirror image. Cassie held hands with it. Garth looked down and away, her dead sister wouldn't let her go. Would it ever be just the two of them?

"I can't." Tears trembled out of Cassie's eyes. "It's the light."

"Don't worry, you'll adjust." He reached down to pull her up, but she stayed put.

"It's too late Cassie." Her sister, Hayley, held her tight.

"It hurts me." Cassie felt the leaching of her skin turning to grey, burning under her clothes. Even the night sky was too much for her burning skin to bear.

The darkness had made its claim. The White Lady had been right. The darkness was more powerful than anyone could imagine. The White Lady had been a vessel and now it had chosen another to take her place.

Cassie collapsed onto the floor. There was nothing Garth could do to help as he watched a sentient cloud of darkness force its way inside Cassie through her mouth.

"Cassie!" The darkness pushed him back. The fight was futile. When the black mist cleared, she was standing upright.

Soon, Cassie would need to feed. She moved back, away from Garth and the outside world. Her skin, cold and calm as the darkness nursed it back to health. The cave was the only safe place for her now.

"I can't go any further." She turned to the shadow form beside her, their hands became entwined. Cassie took a step back as tears ran down her cheeks, her shoulders sinking under defeat. She knew she could never leave.

***

Sienna couldn't find her way out of the caves. Despite being so near to the exit, the darkness was playing tricks on her. There were no more overhead lights running above her head, the floor was uneven and slippery, everywhere were the sounds of dripping water coming from all directions. The floor began to rumble, she was certain she could hear waves crashing nearby. She pushed on; she wasn't going to be afraid anymore. Being on her own afforded her no distractions from the situation she was in. These caves were never-ending. Why wouldn't they let her go? Was this what happened when the last copper nail was hammered into a coffin.

Behind her was the sound of a young girl crying, dripping with cold sea water. Then the crashing thunder of a wave behind them.

"Melanie? Is that you Melanie?" Maura, her dead sister, had been following her trail for years. Ever since her last day on the beach. Wanting her sister back.

Sienna had been running her whole life.

Now her sister had caught up.

"Play with me."

Maura was going to have Sienna all to herself.

Sienna screamed running deeper and deeper into the caves. Her mouth tasted of brine as she slipped. The sound of towering crashing waves followed in quick pursuit.

***

"Please," Garth begged for the final time. It hadn't taken long for Cassie to change. Her skin shone with moonglow. Her black eyes had a cold look in them. He promised to call her an ambulance, but she smiled sadly and shook her head.

"I'm hungry," she kept repeating to Garth. Her hunger caused her great shame. It was for this reason she wouldn't come out. Wouldn't allow Garth to get too close to her.

"I'll pop back home and get you some food." He had to go home. His mother must be frantic with worry. He needed to tell her he was alright.

Cassie looked at him with a lust he couldn't quite comprehend. "I need to feed."

Garth took out his car keys from his bag and jangled them in front of her. "I'll be back in twenty minutes max."

She kept shaking her head. "Leave," she begged over and over. "Don't come back. I need to feed."

He couldn't leave her, not again, she was the one.

He would do anything for her.

***

Weakened by the shuddering of the caves, Bill crawled his way out. He paused briefly to take note of the fresh outside air. His chest was racked with clenching pain.

He took in deep breaths. He needed help. Fiona lived next to the caves. She owed him. The darkness had followed him out, he didn't have much time left, just enough maybe, to find Sandra and talk to her. He staggered to Fiona's house overlooking the caves, a sentry in the darkness. He banged his fist on the door hoping she would be awake. She let him in without a word.

When he saw her in the light, she looked very much younger. Like a fine painting she had been restored to youthful glory. There was a knowing look in her eyes.

"Fiona, something's happened down there. Something big." She raised a hand to silence him.

Fiona smiled. "She's dead." There was joy in her heart that has never been there before.

Bill knew she wasn't referring to Sienna, but of *her*, the creature in the cave. The White Lady was no more.

"She's dead?" But who would take her place?

"We're free?" Bill could barely believe it. He dared to hope. He could finally leave and take that trip to the U.S he'd always dreamed of. He could take Sandra too, they could be together for the rest of their lives. He smiled, suddenly his life seemed his own again.

"I'm free." Fiona pushed him to the floor.

Before he could process what was happening and react, Fiona was on top of him. He could never have anticipated her strength.

In her hand was a dagger which she used to break past his skin. Fiona cracked open his ribcage to the tender heart inside.

She fed.

Inside the mess, his organs were warm and juicy. She went straight for the liver, slippery in her hands. It was the most sumptuous meat she had ever tasted. It simply melted in her mouth and slid down her throat. She ate all of him. It wasn't enough. He would have tasted better if he had been younger, but for the moment it was enough.

She got up and washed her hands. Felt her skin tighten across her body back to her youthful plumpness.

Her son wasn't enough. Neither was Bill. She needed to feed and feed. Only human flesh would do. Garth needed to be dealt with.

She stepped over his carcass, grabbing her coat pausing in the mirror. Now she was radiant, twenty-five again. Her hair black, her eyes blue, her lips plump.

Fiona stepped out into the night. She had the whole of London to feed on.

Life began again.

ABOUT THE AUTHOR

Sarah Budd is a horror writer from London. She has always been fascinated by anything out of the ordinary. Her work has appeared in over twenty magazines and anthologies including *Slash-Her*, *NoSleep Podcast*, *Diabolica Britannica*, *Tales to Terrify*, *Aphotic Realm*, *Sanitarium Magazine*, Dark Fire Fiction, *Mystic Blue Review*, Siren's Call Publications, *Deadman's Tome*, *Innersins*, *Aphelion*, *Bewildering Stories* and *Blood Moon Rising Magazine*.

Twitter: twitter.com/SjbuddJ

Website: http://www.sjbudd.co.uk/

Acknowledgements

A big shout out to Steve and Heather at Brigids Gate Press for all your hard work in making my tale the best version it could be. Carrie Allison-Rolling thanks for being an amazing editor! Thanks to Stephanie Ellis for your proofreading skills and last but not least thank you so much to Elizabeth Leggett for designing my cover. I loved it the moment I saw it!

I'd love to say thank you to all my readers and to all the wonderful people I have met in the Twitter horror community, you've made me feel so welcome. There's simply too many of you to mention!

CONTENT WARNINGS

Suicide, bereavement, implied parental abuse, domestic abuse, kidnap, murder, cannibalism.

MORE FROM BRIGIDS GATE PRESS

Visit our website at: www.brigidsgatepress.com

On the run from a life of prostitution and poverty, exotic dancer Cece Dulac agrees to become the main attraction at an erotic séance hosted by an enigmatic mesmerist, Monsieur Rossignol. As the séance descends into depravity, Cece falls prey to Rossignol's hypnotic power and becomes possessed by a malevolent spirit.

George Dashwood, an aspiring artist, witnesses the séance and fears for Cece. He seeks her out and she seduces him, but she is no longer herself. The spirit controlling her forces her to commit increasingly depraved acts. When the spirit's desire for revenge escalates to murder, George and Cece must find a way to break Rossignol's spell before Cece's soul is condemned forever.

Marionette is an erotic horror novella inspired by traditional folk tales and set in fin de siècle Paris.

A woman develops an unhealthy obsession with a scarecrow. A boy plays with a Ouija board and receives a terrifying warning of murder. A down-on-his-luck father learns what happens when you die in your sleep. These stories and six more frightening tales await the reader within the pages of *Throwing Shadows: A Dark Collec-tion*.

Throwing Shadows will feed that hungry dark side that lives in your cellar.

Arthur, whose life was devastated by the brutal murder of his wife, must come to terms with his diagnosis of dementia. He moves into a new home at a retirement community, and shortly after, has his life turned upside down again when his wife's ghost visits him and sends him on a quest to find her killer so her spirit can move on. With his family and his doctor concerned that his dementia is advancing, will he be able to solve the murder before his independence is permanently restricted?

A Man in Winter examines the horrors of isolation, dementia, loss, and the ghosts that come back to haunt us.

Return to the Weald, the world Stephanie Ellis introduced us to in The Five Turns of the Wheel.

Reborn is the story of Cernunnos, the Father of all, who has risen. Born of blood offerings, he travels to the Layerings—one of those places, like Umbra, which sit just beyond the human veil.

Reborn is the story of Tommy, Betty and Fiddler, the infamous troupe whose bloody rituals were halted by Megan, Tommy's Daughter. Rendered weak by Megan's refusal to allow them to hunt in the human world of the Weald, they seek their rebirth and forgiveness from the Mother and Cernunnos.

Reborn is the story of Megan, who follows Cernunnos and Hweol's sons on a pilgrimage of hope—one that would see her husband restored to her and the dark presence of Hweol removed.

Ultimately, though, Reborn is the story of Betty, the most monstrous of the three brothers. He is Nature, red in tooth and claw. He is what the Mother made him. And who are we to judge?

With Reborn, Ellis delivers another powerful tale of folk horror that will captivate the reader from the first page until its final bloody climax.

Printed in Great Britain
by Amazon